Bradford W. Forbes was telling me about the sensitive nature of a college president's job and there was apparently a lot to say about it. I'd been there twenty minutes and was beginning to wonder if I should tell him his office looked like the front parlor of a Victorian whorehouse. I decided not to.

"Do you see my position, Mr. Spenser," he said and swiveled toward me, leaning forward and putting both his hands palms down on the top of his des. His nails were manicured.

"Yes, sir," I said. "We detectives know how to read people."

Forbes frowned and went on.

"It is a matter of utmost delicacy, Mr. Spenser. I don't know the kind of people who usually employ you, but —"

I interrupted him. "Look, Dr. Forbes, I went to college once. I don't wear my hat indoors. And if a clue comes along and bites me on the ankle I grab it. I am not, however, an Oxford don. I am a private detective. Now, is there something you'd like me to detect or are you just polishing up your elocution for a commencement address?"

Forbes inhaled deeply and let the air out slowly through his nose. "The District Attorney told us you were somewhat overfond of your own wit."

The Godwulf Manuscript
Robert B. Parker

A BERKLEY MEDALLION BOOK
published by
BERKLEY PUBLISHING CORPORATION

This, like everything else, is for
Joan, David, and Daniel.

Houghton Mifflin Company
2 Park Street
Boston, Massachusetts 02107

Library of Congress Catalog Card Number: 73-11404

SBN 425—03967—6

BERKLEY MEDALLION BOOKS are published by
Berkley Publishing Corporation
200 Madison Avenue
New York, N.Y. 10016

BERKLEY MEDALLION BOOK ® TM 757,375

Printed in the United States of America

Berkley Medallion Edition, OCTOBER, 1975

FOURTH PRINTING

A portion of this book appeared in the
October 1973 issue of Argosy.

The office of the university president looked like the front parlor of a successful Victorian whorehouse. It was paneled in big squares of dark walnut, with ornately figured maroon drapes at the long windows. There was maroon carpeting and the furniture was black leather with brass studs. The office was much nicer than the classrooms; maybe I should have worn a tie.

Bradford W. Forbes, the president, was prosperously heavy—reddish face, thick, longish, white hair, heavy white eyebrows. He was wearing a brown pin-striped custom-tailored three-piece suit with a gold Phi Beta Kappa key on a gold watch chain stretched across his successful middle. His shirt was yellow broadcloth and his blue and yellow striped red tie spilled out over the top of his vest.

As he talked, Forbes swiveled his chair around and stared at his reflection in the window. Flakes of the season's first snow flattened out against it, dissolved and trickled down onto the white brick sill. It was very gray out, a November grayness that is peculiar to Boston in late fall, and Forbes's office seemed cheerier than it should have because of that.

He was telling me about the sensitive nature of a college president's job and there was apparently a lot to say about it. I'd been there twenty minutes and my eyes were beginning to cross. I wondered if I should tell him his office looked like a whorehouse. I decided not to.

"Do you see my position, Mr. Spenser," he said and

swiveled back toward me, leaning forward and putting both his hands palms down on the top of his desk. His nails were manicured.

"Yes, sir," I said. "We detectives know how to read people."

Forbes frowned and went on.

"It is a matter of the utmost delicacy, Mr. Spenser—" he was looking at himself in the glass again—"requiring restraint, sensitivity, circumspection, and a high degree of professionalism. I don't know the kind of people who usually employ you, but . . ."

I interrupted him.

"Look, Dr. Forbes, I went to college once, I don't wear my hat indoors. And if a clue comes along and bites me on the ankle I grab it. I am not, however, an Oxford don. I am a private detective. Is there something you'd like me to detect or are you just polishing up your elocution for next year's commencement?"

Forbes inhaled deeply and let the air out slowly through his nose.

"District Attorney Frale told us you were somewhat overfond of your own wit. Tell him, Mr. Tower."

Tower stepped away from the wall where he had been leaning and opened a manila file folder. He was tall and thin, with a Prince Valiant haircut, long sideburns, buckle boots, and a tan gabardine suit. He put one foot on a straight chair and flipped open the folder, no nonsense.

"Carl Tower," he said, "head of campus security. Four days ago a valuable fourteenth-century illuminated manuscript was stolen from our library."

"What is an illuminated manuscript?"

Forbes answered, "A handwritten book, done by monks usually, with illustrations in color, often red and gold in the margins. This particular one is in Latin, and contains an allusion to Richard Rolle, the fourteenth-century English mystic. It was discovered forty years ago behind an ornamental façade at Godwulf Abbey, where it is thought to have been secreted during the pillage of the monasteries which followed Henry the Eighth's break with Rome.''

"Oh," I said, "that illuminated manuscript."

"Right," Tower said briskly. "I can fill you in with description and pictures later. Right now we want to sketch out the general picture. This morning President Forbes received a phone call from someone purporting to represent a campus organization, unnamed. The caller said they had a manuscript and would return it if we would give a hundred thousand dollars to a free school run by an off-campus group."

"So why not do so?"

Again Forbes answered. "We don't have one hundred thousand dollars, Mr. Spenser."

I looked around. "Perhaps you could rent out the south end of your office for off-street parking," I said.

Forbes closed his eyes for perhaps ten seconds, inhaled audibly, and then went on.

"All universities lose money. This one, large, urban, in some way undistinguished, loses more than most. We have little alumni support, and that which we do have is often from the less affluent segments of our culture. We do not have one hundred thousand dollars."

I looked at Tower. "Can the thing be fenced?"

"No, its value is historical and literary. The only market would be another university, and they would recognize it at once."

"There is another problem, Mr. Spenser. The manuscript must be kept in a controlled environment. Airconditioned, proper humidity, that sort of thing. Should it be kept out of its case too long it will fall apart. The loss to scholarship would be tragic." Forbes' voice sank at the last sentence. He examined a fleck of cigar ash on his lapel, then brought his eyes up level with mine and stared at me steadily.

"Can we count on you, Mr. Spenser? Can you get it back?"

"Win this one for the Gipper," I said.

Behind me Tower gave a kind of snort and Forbes looked as if he'd found half a worm in his apple.

"I beg your pardon," he said.

"I'm thirty-seven years old and short on rah-rah, Dr. Forbes. If you'll pay me, and do your Pat O'Brien impressions somewhere else, I'll see if I can find the manuscript."

"This gets us nowhere," Tower said. "Let me take him down to my office, Dr. Forbes, and lay it all out for him. I know the situation and I'm used to dealing with people like him."

Forbes nodded without speaking. As we left the office he was standing at his window, hands clasped behind his back, looking at the snow.

The administration building was cinder block, with vinyl tile, frosted glass partitions, two tones of green on the corridor walls. Tower's office was six doors down from Forbes's and not much bigger than Forbes's desk. It was done in beige metal. Tower got seated behind his desk and tapped his teeth with a pencil.

"It's really slick how you can charm a client, Spenser."

I sat across from him in the other chair. I didn't say anything.

"Sure," he said, "the old man's kind of a ham, but he's a damn good administrator, and a damn fine person."

"Okay," I said, "he's terrific. When I grow up I want to be just like him. What about the Godwulf Manuscript?"

"Right." He took an eight-by-ten color print from his

4

manila folder and handed it to me. It showed an elegantly handwritten book lying open on a table. The words were in Latin and around the margins in bright red and gold were drawn knights and ladies and lions on their hind legs, and vines and stags and a serpentine dragon being lanced by an armor-clad hero on a plump and feminine horse. The first letter at the top left on each page was elaborately drawn and incorporated into the design of the margins.

"It was taken three nights ago from its case in the library's rare book room. The watchman punched in there at two and again at four. At four he found the case open and the manuscript gone. He can't say positively that it wasn't there at two but he assumes he would have noticed. It's hard to prove you didn't see something. You want to talk to him?"

"No," I answered. "That's routine stuff. You or the cops can do that as well as I could. Have you got a suspect?"

"SCACE."

"SCACE?"

"Student Committee Against Capitalist Exploitation. Revolution at the far-left fringe of the spectrum. I don't know it the way courts want it known; I know it the way you know things like that if you're in my line of work."

"Informer?"

"Not really, though I've got some contacts. Mostly though it's a gut guess. It's the kind of thing they'd do. I've been here for five years. Before that I was with the Bureau for ten. I've spent a lot of time on radicals and I've developed a feel for them."

"Like the late director developed a feel for them?"

"Hoover? No, he's one reason I quit the Bureau. He was a hell of a cop once but his time came and went before he died. I got enough feel about the radical kids not to classify them. The worst of them have the same things wrong that zealots always have, but you can't blame them for getting rigid about some of the things that go on. That ain't Walt Disney World out there." He nodded out his window at the blacktop quadrangle where the slush was beginning to collect in semi-fluid patterns as the kids sloshed through it. A thin and leafless sapling leaned against its support stake. It was a long way from home.

"Where do I find SCACE? Do they have a clubhouse with college pennants on the wall and old Pat Boone records playing day and night?"

"Not hardly," Tower said. "Your best bet would be to talk to the secretary, Terry Orchard. She's the least unpleasant of them, and the least unreasonable."

"Where do I find her?"

Tower pressed down an intercom button and asked someone to bring him in the SCACE file.

"We keep a file on all college organizations. Just routine. We're not singling SCACE out."

"I bet you've got a thick one on the Newman club," I said.

"Okay, we don't pay as much attention to some as others, granted. But we're not persecuting anybody."

Tower's door opened and a post-co-ed blonde in high white boots came in. She was wearing something in purple suede that was too short for a skirt and too long for a belt. Above that was a scarlet satin long-collared shirt with puffed sleeves and a deep neck. Her thighs were a little heavy—but perhaps she thought the same of me. She laid a thick brown file folder on Tower's desk, looked me over like the weight guesser at a fair, and left.

"Who was that," I asked, "the dean of women?"

Tower was thumbing through the file. He extracted a typewritten sheet.

"Here," he said and handed it across. It was a file on Terry Orchard: Home address, Newton, Mass. College address, none. Transient.

"Transient?" I said.

"Yeah, she drifts. Mostly she lives with a guy named Dennis Powell, who's some kind of SCACE official. She also used to live sometimes with a girl over on Hemenway Street. Connelly, Catherine Connelly. It's all there in the file."

"Yeah, and the file is a year old."

"I don't have the staff. The kids come and go. They're only here four years, if that. The real romantic radicals like to think of themselves as free floaters, street people. They sleep around on floors and sofas and Christ knows where else. Your best bet would be to get her after class."

Again the intercom, again came purple skirt.

"See if you can get Terry Orchard's schedule from the registrar's office for me, Brenda." All business. Competent. Professional. No hanky-panky. No wonder he lasted ten years with the Feds.

She was back in about five minutes with a Xeroxed copy of an IBM print-out of Terry Orchard's schedule. She had a class in the psychology of repression that ended at three in Hardin Hall, fourth floor. It was 2:35.

"Picture?" I asked Tower.

"Right here," he said. He looked at the massive watch on the broad snakeskin band that he wore. It was the kind they call a chronometer, which will tell you not only the time but the atmospheric pressure and the lunar cycle.

"Three o'clock," he said. "Plenty of time; Hardin Hall is two buildings away across the quad. Take the elevator to the fourth floor. Room four-o-nine is to your left about two doors down the corridor."

I looked at the picture. It wasn't good. Obviously an ID shot. Square face, rather thick lips, and hair pulled tight back away from her face. She looked older than the twenty her file had said she was. But most people do in ID shots. I reserved judgment.

7

"Okay," I said. "I'll go see her. How about a retainer? Forbes telling me how indigent you all were has me nervous."

"One will come to you in the mail from the comptroller. A week's worth in advance."

"Sold," I said. I gave him back the file and the picture.

"Don't you want it?"

"I'll remember," I said. We shook hands. I left.

The corridors were beginning to fill with students changing classes. I pushed through into the quadrangle. The thin elm sapling I'd seen from Forbes's window wasn't as lonely as I thought. Five cousins, no less spindly, were geometrically spaced about the hot top quadrangle. Three sides of the quadrangle were bordered with gray-white brick buildings. Each had wide stairs leading up to multiple glass-door banks. The buildings were perfectly square, four stories high, with gray painted casement windows. It looked like corporate headquarters for White Tower Hamburgers. The fourth side opened onto the street, where MBTA trains rumbled.

Under one of the saplings a boy and girl sat close together. He was wearing black sneakers and brown socks, flared dungarees, a blue denim shirt and a fatigue jacket with staff sergeant's stripes, a Seventh Division patch, and the name tag Gagliano. His thick black hair blossomed out from his head in a Caucasian afro and the snow streaked the rose-colored lenses of his gold-rimmed glasses. The girl had on bib overalls and a quilted ski parka. On her feet were blue suede hiking boots with thick corrugated soles and silver lacing studs. Her blond hair was perfectly straight and halfway to her waist. She wore a woven leather headband to keep it out of her eyes. I wondered if it was a mark of advancing years when you no longer wanted to neck in the snow.

A black kid in a Borsalino hat came out of the library across the quadrangle. He had on a red sleeveless jumpsuit, black shirt with bell sleeves, high-heeled black patent leather boots with black laces. A full-length black leather trench coat hung open. A Fu Manchu mustache swept to the chin on each side of his mouth. Two kids in football jackets exchanged looks as he went by. They had necks like pilot whales. A slim black girl in an Angela Davis haircut and huge pendant earrings trailed a gentle scent of imported bath soap past me as I went into Hardin Hall, the third building on the quadrangle.

The elevator that took me to the fourth floor was covered with obscene graffiti that some proprietous soul had tried to doctor into acceptability, so that phrases like "buck you" mingled with the more traditional expletives. It was a losing cause, but that didn't make it a bad one.

Room 409 had a blond oak door with a window in it, just like the other six classrooms that lined the corridor on each side. Inside I could see about forty kids facing a woman seated up front at a table. She wore a dark maroon silk granny dress with a low scooped neckline. The dress was covered with an off-white floral design that looked like hydrangea. Her long black hair was caught back with a gold barrette. She wore large round horn-rimmed glasses, and was smoking a corncob pipe with a curved amber stem. She was speaking with great animation and her hands flashed with large rings as she spoke and gestured. A number of students were taking notes, some watched her closely, some had their heads down on the desk and were apparently asleep. Terry Orchard was there, back row, looking out the window at the snow. She looked like kids I'd seen before, the real goods, faded Levi jacket and pants, faded and unironed denim shirt, hair pulled back tight in a pigtail like an eighteenth-century British sailor. No make-up, no jewelry. On her feet were yellow leather work shoes that laced up over the ankle. She wasn't built so you could tell from where I was, but I would have bet my retainer that she wouldn't be wearing a bra. There are kids that get their anti-establishment milkman's overalls in the Marsha Jordan Shop with their own charge card. But Terry wasn't one of them. Her clothes exclaimed their origin in Jerry's Army-Navy Store. She was better-looking than her picture, but still looked older than twenty.

• 2 •

The bell rang and the teacher stopped—apparently in midsentence—put her corncob pipe in her mouth, folded up her notes, and started out. The kids followed. Terry Orchard was one of the first out the door. I fell in beside her.

"Excuse me," I said, "Miss Orchard?"

"Yes?" No hostility, but very little warmth either.

"My name is Spenser and I'd like to buy you lunch."

"Why?"

"How about, I'm a Hollywood producer casting for a new movie?"

"Get lost," she said without looking at me.

"How about, if you don't come to lunch with me I'll break both your thumbs and you'll never play pool again?"

She stopped and looked at me. "Look," she said, "What the hell do you want anyway? Why don't you go hang around down the convent school with a bag of candy bars?"

We were down one flight of stairs now and turning toward the next flight. I took a card out of the breast pocket of my jacket and handed it to her. She read it.

"Oh, for crissake," she said. "A private eye? Jesus. Is that corny! Are you going to pull a gat on me? Did my old man send you?"

"Miss Orchard, look at it this way, you get a free lunch and half a million laughs afterward talking to the gang back at the malt shop. I get a chance to ask some questions, and if you answer them I'll let you play with my handcuffs. If you don't answer them, you still get the lunch. Who else has been out with a private eye lately?''

"A pig is a pig," she said. "Whether he's public or private, he works for the same people."

"Next time you're in trouble," I said, "call a hippie."

"Oh, crap, you know damn well . . ."

I stopped her. "I know damn well that it would be easier to argue over lunch. My fingernails are clean and I promise to use silverware. I'm paying with establishment expense money. It's a chance to exploit them."

She almost smiled. "Okay," she said. We'll go to the Pub. They'll let me in dressed this way. And this is the only way I dress."

We had reached the ground level and headed out into the quadrangle. We then turned left out onto the avenue. The buildings around the university were old red brick. Many of the windows were boarded, and few of the rest had curtains. Along the avenue was some of the detritus that gathers at the exterior edge of a big university: used-book shops, cut-rate clothing stores featuring this year's freaky fashion, a porno shop, a school of astrology-reading in a storefront, a term-paper mill, three sub joints, hamburgers, pizza, fried chicken, a place selling soft ice cream. The porno shop was bigger than the book-store.

The Pub was probably once a gas station. It had been painted entirely antique green, glass windows and all. The word Pub was gold-leafed on the door. Inside were a juke box, a color TV, dark wooden tables and high-backed booths, a bar along one side. The ceiling was low and most of the light came from a big Budweiser sign in the rear. The bar was mostly empty in midafternoon; a group in one booth was playing cards. In the back a boy and girl were talking very softly to one another. Terry Orchard and I took the second booth from the door. The table top was covered with initials scratched with penknife and pencil point over a long period of time. The upholstery of the booth was torn in places and cracked in others.

"Do you recommend anything?" I asked.

"The corned beef is okay," she said.

A fat, tough, tired-looking waitress wearing sneakers came for our order. I ordered us both a corned beef sandwich and a beer. Terry Orchard lit a cigarette and blew smoke through her nostrils.

"If I drink that beer you're an accomplice. I'm under twenty-one," she said.

"That's okay, it gives me a chance to show contempt for the establishment."

The waitress set down two large schooners of draft beer. "Your sandwiches will be out in a minute," she said, and shuffled off. Terry took a sip.

I said, "You're under arrest." Her eyes flared open, and then she smiled, grudgingly, over the glass.

"You're nowhere near as funny as you think you are, Mr. Spenser, but you're a hell of a lot better than I figured. What do you want?"

"I'm looking for the Godwulf Manuscript. The university president himself called me in, showed me his profile, dazzled me with his elocution, and assigned me to get it back. Tower, the campus cop, suggested you might help me."

"What is a Godwulf Manuscript?"

"It's an illuminated manuscript from the fourteenth century. It was in the rare book room at your library; now it isn't. It's being held for ransom by an unidentified campus group."

"Why did Super Swine think I could help?"

"Super Swine—you must be an English major—he thought you could help because he thinks SCACE took it and you are the secretary of that organization."

"Why does he think SCACE took it?"

13

"Because he has an instinct for it, and maybe because he knows something. He's not just a storefront clothes-horse. When he's not getting his nails manicured and his hair styled with a razor, he is probably a pretty shrewd cop. He didn't tell me everything he knows."

"Why not?"

"Sweetie, no one ever tells me everything he knows; it is the nature of the beast."

"You must get a swell view of life looking at it through a keyhole half the time."

"I see what's there."

The waitress brought our sandwiches, large, on dark bread, with pickles and chips. They were sweet pickles, though. I ordered two more beers.

"What about the manuscript?" I asked.

"I don't know anything about it."

"Okay," I said, "tell me about SCACE, then."

Her face was less friendly now. "Why do you want to know about SCACE?"

"I won't know till I've learned. That's my line of work. I ask about things. And people don't tell me anything so I ask about more things, and so on. Now and then things fall into place."

"Well, there's nothing to fall into place here. We're a revolutionary organization. We are trying to develop a new consciousness, we're committed to social change, to redistribution of wealth, to real liberty for everyone, not just for the bosses and the rip-off artists."

Her voice had become almost mechanical, like the people who do telephone canvassing for dance studios. I wondered how long it had been since she'd actually thought about all those words and what they really meant.

"How you go about getting these things instituted?"

"By continuous social pressure. By pamphleteering, by marching, by demonstrating our support for all causes which crack the establishment's united front. By refusing to accede to anything that benefits the establishment. By opposing injustice whenever we find it.''

"Making much progress?" I asked.

"You bet your life. We're growing every day. There were only three or four of us at first. Now there are five times that many."

"No, I meant injustice."

She was silent, looking at me.

"I haven't made much progress that way either," I said.

A tall, big-boned blond kid wearing a plaid shirt and Levis came into the Pub and looked around. He was clean-shaven and wild-haired, and when his eyes got used to the dimness he headed over to us and slid in beside Terry Orchard. He picked up her half-filled glass, drained it, set it down, and said to her, "Who's this creep?"

"Dennis," she said, "be nice."

He squeezed her arm hard with one hand and repeated the question. I answered for her.

"My name's Spenser."

He turned his head toward me and looked very hard at me. "I'm talking to her, not you, Jack. Shut up."

"Dennis!" She said it with more emphasis this time. "Who the hell do you think you are? Let go of my arm."

I reached over and took hold of his wrist. "Listen, Goldilocks," I said, "I bought her a beer and you drank it. On my block that entitles you to get your upper lip fattened."

He yanked his hand away from me. "You think maybe the long hair makes me soft?"

"Dennis," Terry said, "he's a private detective."

"Freaking pig," he said, and swung at me. I pulled my head out of the way and slipped out of the booth. The punch rammed against the back of the booth, the kid swore and turned toward me. He was not planning to quit, so I figured it best end swiftly. I feinted toward his stomach

15

with my left hand, then hooked it over his lowered guard and turned my whole shoulder into it as it connected on the side of his face. He sat down hard on the floor.

Terry Orchard went down on her knees beside him, her arms around his shoulders.

"Don't get up, Dennis. Stay there. He'll hurt you."

"She's right, kid," I said. "You're an amateur. I do this kind of thing for a living."

The big old tough waitress came around and said, "What the hell is going on? You want the cops in here? You want to fight, go outside."

"No more trouble," I said. "I'm a movie stunt man and I was just showing my friend how to slip a punch."

"And I'm Wonder Woman and if you do it again I'm calling the blues." She stomped off.

"The beer offer still holds," I said. The kid got up, his jaw already beginning to puff. He wouldn't want to chew much tomorrow. He sat down in the booth beside Terry, who still held his arm protectively.

"I'm sorry, Mr. Spenser," she said. "He isn't really like that."

"What's he really like?" I asked.

His eyes, which had been a little out of focus, were sharpening. "I'm like I am," he said. "And I don't like to see Terry sitting around boozing with some nosy goddamn gumshoe. What are you doing around here anyway?"

The left hook had taken some of the starch out of him. His voice was less assertive, more petulant. But it hadn't made him any sweeter.

"I'm a private detective looking for a stolen rare book, the Godwulf Manuscript. Ever hear of it?"

"No."

"How'd you know I was a private cop?"

"I didn't till Terry said so, but you got the look. If your hair were much shorter it would be a crew cut. In

16

the movement you learn to be suspicious. Besides, Terry's my woman."

"I'm not anybody's woman, Dennis. That's a sexist statement. I'm not a possession."

"Oh, Christ," I said. "Could we cut the polemics a minute. If you know of the manuscript, know this also. It has to be kept in a climate-controlled atmosphere. Otherwise it will disintegrate. And then it will be worthless both to scholars and to you, or whoever the book-nappers may be. The university hasn't got the money to ransom it."

"They got the money to buy football players and build a hockey rink and pay goddamn professors to teach three hours a week and write books the rest of the time."

"I'm not into educational reform this week. Do you have any thoughts on where the missing manuscript might be?"

"If I did I wouldn't tell you. If I didn't I could find out, and when I found out I wouldn't tell you then either. You aren't peeking over the transom in some flophouse now, snoopy. You're on a college campus and you stick out like a sore thumb. You will find out nothing at all because no one will tell you. You and the other dinosaurs can rut around all you want—we're not buying it."

"Buying what?"

"Whatever you're selling. You are the other side, man."

"We aren't getting anywhere," I said. "I'll see you."

I left a five on the table to cover the lunch and left. It was getting dark now and the commuter traffic was starting. I felt the beer a little, and I felt the sadness of kids like that who weren't buying it and weren't quite sure what it was. I got my car from where I'd parked it by a hydrant. It had a parking ticket tied to the windshield wiper. Eternal vigilance, I thought, is the price of liberty. I tore the ticket up and drove home.

17

• 3 •

I was living that year on Marlborough Street, two blocks up from the Public Garden. I made myself hash and eggs for supper and read the morning's *New York Times* while I ate. I took my coffee with me into the living room and tried looking at television. It was awful so I shut it off and got out my carving. I'd been working on a block of hard pine for about six months now, trying to reproduce in wood the bronze statue of an Indian on horseback that stands in front of the Museum of Fine Arts. The wood was so hard that I had to sharpen the knives every time I worked. And I spent about half an hour this night with whetstone and file before I began on the pine. At eleven I turned on the news, watched it as I undressed, shut it off, and went to bed.

At some much later time, in the dark, the phone rang. I spiraled slowly upward from sleep and answered it after it had rung for what seemed a long time. The girl's voice at the other end was thick and very slow, almost like a 45 record played at 33.

"Spenser?"

"Yeah."

"It's Terry . . . help me."

"Where are you?"

"Eighty Hemenway Street, apartment three."

"Ten minutes," I said, and rolled out of bed.

It was 3:05 in the morning when I got into my car and headed for Hemenway Street. It wasn't 3:15 when I got there. Three A.M. traffic in Boston is rarely a serious problem.

Hemenway Street, on the other hand, often is. It is a short street of shabby apartment buildings, near the university, and for no better reason than Haight-Ashbury had, or the East Village, it had become the place for street people. On the walls of the building Maoist slogans were scrawled in red paint. On a pillar at the entrance to the street was a proclamation of Gay Liberation. There were various recommendations about pigs being offed scrawled on the sidewalk. I left my car double-parked outside 80 Hemenway and tried the front door. It was locked. There were no doorbells to push. I took my gun out, reversed it, and broke the blass with the handle. Then I reached around and turned the dead lock and opened the door from the inside.

Number 3 was down the hall, right rear. There were bicycles with tire locks lining both walls, and some indeterminate litter behind them. Terry's door was locked. I knocked; no answer. I knocked again and heard something faint, like the noise of a kitten. The corridor was narrow. I braced my back against the wall opposite the door and drove my heel, with 195 pounds behind it, against the door next to the knob. The inside jamb splintered, and the door tore open and banged violently against the wall as it opened.

Inside all the lights were on. The first thing I saw was Dennis Goldilocks lying on his back with his mouth open, his arms outspread, and a thick patch of tacky and blackening blood covering much of his chest. Near him on her hands and knees was Terry Orchard. Her hair was loose and falling forward as though she were trying to dry it in the sun. But it wasn't sunny in there. She wore only a pajama top with designs of Snoopy and the Red Baron on it, and it was from her that the faint kitten sounds were coming. She swayed almost rhythmically back and forth making no progress, moving in no direction, just swaying and mewing. Between her and Dennis on the floor was a small white-handled gun. It or something had been fired in the room; I could smell it.

I knelt beside the blond boy and felt for the big pulse in his neck. The minute I touched his skin I knew I'd never feel the pulse. He was cool already and getting colder. I turned to Terry. She still swayed, head down and sick. I could smell something vaguely medicinal on her breath. Her breath was heaving and her eyes were slits. I pulled her to her feet, and held her, one arm around her back. She was almost all the way under. I couldn't tell from what, but whatever it was, it was an o.d.

I walked her into the bathroom, got her pajama shirt off, and got her under the shower. I turned the water on warm and then slowly to full cold and held her under. She quivered and struggled faintly. The sleeves of my jacket were wet up past the elbows and my shirtfront was soaked through. She pushed one hand weakly at my face and began to cry instead of mew. I held her there some more. As I held her I kept listening for footsteps behind me. The door had made a hell of a lot of noise when I kicked it open, and the gunshot must have been a loud one long before that. But the neighborhood was not, apparently, that kind of neighborhood. Not the kind to look into gunshots and doors splintering and such. The kind to pull the covers up over the head and burrow the face in the pillow and say screw it. Better him than me.

I got a hand up to her neck and felt her pulse. It was quicker—I guessed about sixty. I got her out of the shower and across to the bedroom. I didn't see a robe, so I pulled the blanket off the bed and wrapped it around her. Then we waltzed to the kitchen. I got water boiling and found some instant coffee and a cup. She was babbling now, nothing coherent, but the words were intelligible. I made coffee with her balanced half over one hip, my arm around her and the blanket caught in my fist to keep her warm. Then

20

back to the living room to the day bed—there were no chairs in the kitchen—and sat her down.

She pushed aside the coffee and spilled some on herself and cried out at the pain, but I got her to drink some. And again some. And one more time. Her eyes were open now and her breath was much less shallow. I could see her rib cage swell and settle regularly beneath the blanket. She finished the coffee.

I stood her up and we began to walk back and forth across the apartment, which wasn't much of a walk. There were the living room, a small bedroom, a bath, and a kitchenette, barely big enough to stand in. The living room, in which the quick and dead were joined, held only a card table, a steamer trunk with a lamp on it, and the studio couch on whose bare mattress Terry Orchard had drunk her coffee. The blanket I had pulled off the bed had been its only adornment, and as I looked into the bedroom I could see a cheap deal bureau beside the bed. On it was a candle stuck in a Chianti bottle beneath a bare light bulb hanging from a ceiling.

I looked down at Terry Orchard. There were tears running down her cheeks, and less of her weight leaned on me.

"Sonova bitch," she said. "Sonova bitch, sonova bitch, sonova bitch."

"When you can talk to me, talk to me. Till then keep walking," I said.

She just kept saying sonova bitch, in a dead singsong voice, and I found that as we walked we were keeping time to the curse, *left, right, sonova bitch.* I realized that the broken door was still wide open and as we sonova-bitched by on the next swing I kicked it shut with my heel. A few more turns and she fell silent, then she said, half question—

"Spenser?"

"Yeah."

"Oh my God, Spenser."

"Yeah."

We stopped walking and she turned against me with her face hard against my chest. She clenched onto my shirt with both fists and seemed to be trying to blend into me. We stood motionless like that for a long time. Me with my arms around her. Both wet and dripping and the dead boy with his wide sightless eyes not looking at us.

"Sit down," I said after a while. "Drink some more coffee. We have to talk."

She didn't want to let go of me, but I pried her off and sat her on the day bed. She huddled inside the blanket, her wet hair plastered down around her small head, while I made some more coffee.

We sat together on the day bed, sipping coffee. I had the impulse to say, "What's new?" but squelched it. Instead I said, "Tell me about it, now."

"Oh God, I can't."

"You have to."

"I want to get out of here. I want to run."

"Nope. You have to sit here and tell me what happened. From the very first thing that happened to the very last thing that happened. And you have to do it now, because you are in very big trouble and I have to know exactly how big."

"Trouble? Jesus, you think I shot him, don't you?"

"The thought occurred to me."

"I didn't shoot him. They shot him. The ones that made me take the dope. The ones that made me shoot the gun."

"Okay, but start with the first thing. Whose apartment is this?"

"Ours, Dennis's and mine." She nodded at the floor and then started and looked away quickly.

"Dennis is Dennis Powell, right?"

"Yes."

"And you live together and are not married, right?"

"Yes."

"When did the people come who did this?"

"I don't know exactly, it was late, about two-thirty maybe."

"Who were they?"

"I don't know. Two men. Dennis seemed to know them."

"What did they do?"

"They knocked on the door. Dennis got up, we weren't asleep, we never go to sleep till very late, and asked, 'Who is it?' I couldn't hear what they said. But he let them in. That's why I think he knew them. When he opened the door they came in very fast. One of them pushed him against the wall and the other one came into the bedroom and dragged me out of bed. Neither one said anything. Dennis said something like, 'Hey, what's the idea?' or 'Hey, what's going on?' One of them had a gun and he held it on both of us. He never said anything. Neither one. It was spooky. The other guy reached in his coat pocket and came out with my gun."

"Is that your gun on the floor?" I asked.

She wouldn't look but nodded.

"Okay, then what?" I asked.

"He handed my gun to the first man, the man with the gun, and then he grabbed me and turned me around and put his hand over my mouth and bent my arm up behind me and the other man shot Dennis twice."

"With your gun?"

"Yes."

"Then what?"

"Then—" She paused and closed her eyes and shook her head.

"Go on," I said.

"Then the man that shot Dennis made me hold the gun in my hand and shoot it into Dennis. He held my wrist and

23

squeezed my finger on the trigger." She said it in a rush and the words nearly ran together.

"Did he have on gloves?"

She thought a minute. "Yes, yellow ones, I think they might have been rubber or plastic."

"Then what?"

"Then the one who was holding me made me lie down on the bed. I didn't have anything on but my top. And the other one poured some kind of dope in my mouth and forced it shut and held my nose till I swallowed it. Then they just held me there with a hand over my mouth for a little while, then they left."

I didn't say anything. If she invented that story coming out of a narcotic coma she was some kind of special species and nothing I could handle. She might have hallucinated the whole thing, depending on what she had taken. Or the story might be true.

"Why did they make me shoot him after he was dead?" she asked.

I discovered as I answered that I believed her. "To hook you on a paraffin test. When you fire a handgun cordite particles impregnate your skin. A lab man puts paraffin over it, lets it dry, peels it off, and tests it. The particles show up in the wax."

It took a minute to register. "A lab man, you mean the police?"

"Yes, honey, the police."

"No, can't we get out of here? I'll go home. You won't say anything. My father will pay you. He has money. I know he can give you some . . ."

"Your boy friend, dead in your apartment, killed with your gun, you gone? They'd come and get you and bring you back. Do you know a lawyer?"

"A lawyer, how the hell would I know a freaking lawyer?" She looked desperately toward the door. "I'm splitting, screw this scene." Her voice had gotten harsh and tough with fright, and I noticed her lapse into the jargon of her peer group as her fright increased. When she'd been clinging to me she talked like a young girl in college. When she wanted to get away from me her voice and language changed. I held her against me with my arm around her shoulder.

"Listen," I said. "You are in trouble enough to pull up over your head and tie a knot in. But you're not in it alone. I'll help you. It's my line of work. I'll get you a lawyer in a bit. Then I'll call the cops. Before I do, though—" She started to speak and I squeezed her. "Listen," I said. "When the cops come don't say anything, don't talk to them, don't argue with them, don't be hostile, don't be smart. Do not say anything to anybody till you talk to the lawyer. His name is Vincent Haller. He'll see you soon after you go downtown. Talk only with him present and say only what he says you should. Have you ever been busted?"

"No."

"Okay. It's not anywhere near as bad as you think it is. No one will hurt you. No one will grab you under a bright light and hit you with a hose. You'll be okay and you won't be in long. Haller will take care of you."

She nodded. I went on.

"Before I make my call—do you have any idea why the men did this?"

"No."

"Do you use drugs?"

"Yes."

"Do you know what they gave you?"

"No. It tasted like paregoric and smelled like ether. It wasn't anything I'd tried. Whatever it was, was a downer though."

"Okay. Get dressed. I'm going to call."

The first of Boston's finest to arrive were two bulls from a radio car. They came in, told us not to touch anything, got our names, frisked me, took my gun, and looked closely at us till the homicide people came. They came, as they always do, in large numbers: technicians, photographers, someone from the medical examiner's. Two guys in white coats to carry out the corpse and some dicks to investigate the crime and question the suspects. In this case the crew was led by the commander of the homicide bureau, Lt. Martin Quirk. I'm 6'1'' and he was taller than I was, taller and thicker. His hands and fingers were thick and his lips were thick and his nose was broad. His thick black hair was cut close. He was clean-shaven at 4 A.M. and his shoes gleamed with dark polish. His shirt was freshly ironed and his tie neatly knotted. His suit was immaculate and sharply creased. He wore a Tyrolean hat with a feather in it and a white raincoat, which he never took off. His face was pockmarked and there was a short scar at one corner of his mouth.

He stood now looking at me with his raincoat open and his hands in his hip pockets. "This is sure a lucky break for us, Spenser, having you on this to help us out. We need slick professionals like yourself to straighten us out and all. Keep us from forgetting to look for fingerprints, missing clues, and stuff."

"I didn't plan to get into this, Lieutenant. The kid called me for help and I came over and found her. And him. She was badly drugged. I got her sobered up a little and called you.''

"How did she know you?" Quirk asked.

"I'm on a case that she's involved in."

"What case?"

"Looking for a rare missing manuscript stolen from a university.''

"What university?"

"If it seems pertinent, I'll tell you."

"If I want to know you'll tell me." Quirk's voice squeezed out sharp and flat like sheet metal.

"I'll tell you if you need to know it. I don't make a living telling cops everything they want to know about clients.''

"I don't make a living taking crap from hole-in-the-wall shysters like you, Spenser.''

A thin, blue-jowled sergeant named Belson drifted in between Quirk and me.

"Come on, Lieutenant, this don't get us far. Both the girl and the victim are university students and there's a fair bet that it's the same university that hired Spenser.''

Quirk looked at me, then Belson. "Do you know him?" he asked, nodding at me.

"Yeah, he used to work out of the Suffolk County D.A.'s office about five years ago. I hear he got canned.''

"Okay, get his story." He turned to me. "You're not working for the D.A. now, boy, you're working my side of the street, and if you get in my way I'll kick your ass right into the gutter. Got that?''

"Can I feel your muscle?" I said.

Quirk looked at me without saying anything, then turned away and walked over to the girl.

Belson shook his head and pulled out a notebook.

"Start up with the lieutenant, Spenser, and you'll end up looking like you went through a pepper mill.''

"I won't be able to sleep without a night light," I said.

Belson shrugged. "Okay. Start from the beginning. You're in the business. I don't have to lead you."

I told him, omitting, mostly from stubbornness, the name of my client, including, because it was sure to come out anyway, the incident in the Pub that afternoon, when I had knocked the kid down.

Belson shook his head again. "How could anyone get mad at a sweetheart like you? I would have thought he'd have been hypnotized with the way you're so agreeable."

I let that go.

"You're sure you might not have been hustling his chick just a little, Spenser? And maybe you were over here hustling her again and he came home and caught you, and an argument developed?"

"Yeah, and I pulled out my fourteen-dollar Saturday night special and let fly at him. Come off it, Belson. You're just talking for the hell of it. You know I didn't do it. You know I wouldn't use a piece of cheap tin like that gun. If I had, you know I would have covered it better than this."

"Okay, maybe I don't like you for it. I've known you a long time and it's not your style. But it could happen. you got nothing against girls, I can recall. It could be his gun and you had to take it away from him and it went off. Lotta people get killed by people in a way that ain't their style."

"And I shot him four times in the chest getting it away from him?"

"Could be to cover it up, make it look different."

"You're fishing, Frank," I said.

"Maybe."

"Have you heard the girl's story yet?"

"Nope, lieutenant's getting that now."

"He's going to love it," I said.

"Of course you got it before you called us," Belson said.

"She was way under from something. I had to bring her out."

"And then you had to ask her what happened and then she had to tell you. And then you had to fix up a story maybe."

"Wait till you hear the story. You don't think I'm smart enough to work up something like that. You guys are cops, not priests. Calling you isn't a ritual act. I called you as soon as my judgment told me it was both feasible and prudent."

Belson set fire to a half-smoked cigar before he said anything. Then he said, "You talk good for a dumb slug; feasible and prudent, my, my."

From the other side of the room Quirk spoke over his shoulder without turning his head. "Belson, bring the private license over here."

Belson nodded me toward Quirk and I walked over. Quirk was straddling the only straight chair in the room, with his forearms crossed on the back. Before him Terry Orchard was on the couch. She had on a denim shirt and Levis again, but her hair was still wet and tight on her skull. She looked awfully small.

"Spenser," he said without looking up. "She says she won't say anything unless you say it's all right. She says you told her not to talk to us without a lawyer."

"Right enough, Lieutenant. I knew you wouldn't want to take advantage of her when she was confused, or perhaps in a state of shock."

"We're going to take her in."

"I thought you might."

"We'd like you to come along, too," Quirk said.

"I wouldn't miss it," I said.

Terry looked at me with her eyes very wide and dark. I said to her, "Haller will be there. Just do as I said."

29

The assistant M.E., a small man with thick glasses and gray curly hair, came over to Quirk.

"I'm through," he said. "If you are too we'll haul him off."

"Any opinions, Manny?" Quirk asked.

"Yeah, I'd guess he was shot in the chest."

"That med school training really gives you insight," Quirk said. "Anything that I need to know that you can tell me now?"

"Shot sometime in the last five or six hours, cause of death presumable gunshot. I don't see any other signs. Got any corroborative testimony?"

Quirk looked at Belson.

"Spenser says the kid was dead when he arrived at three-fifteen and that the blood had gotten tacky and the skin was cool," Belson said.

The assistant M.E. said, "That seems about right, but it could be a couple hours earlier for all I can prove here."

Quirk nodded. "Okay, thanks, Manny." And then to the two white-coated interns, "Take him away."

They bundled Dennis Powell onto the stretcher. He'd already started to stiffen and he was getting awkward to handle. They straightened his arms out down by his side, put his ankles together, wrapped the tarp around him, and strapped him into the stretcher. Then they dollied him out. They had to stand him up to get him out the apartment door, and when they did the top of him lolled against the straps. Terry made a noise and looked away. The stretcher bumped down the stairs and out to the ambulance. A few curious early risers stood around staring. The two harness bulls who'd showed up first kept them away from the door. A little fat dick in a long blue overcoat with a button missing came in after letting the stretcher out.

"Nothing, Lieutenant. Nobody heard nothing, nobody

saw nothing, nobody knows nothing. Half of them are goddamn faggots anyway.''

''Jesus Christ,'' Quirk said. ''Just give me information; don't review the witnesses' sex life for me.''

''Okay, Lieutenant. I mean I figured that being as they was faggots you might not want to take their word. You know how these goddamn perverts are.''

''No, I don't know, and I don't want you to tell me. Stay around, ask questions. See what you can find out about these two. Try to remember you're on the homicide squad, not the vice squad. When I want a fag count, I'll let you know.''

The dick hustled out. Quirk shook his head. Belson was looking up at the ceiling, puffing the cigar butt that was barely clearing his lips by now.

''Take 'em downtown, Frank,'' Quirk said to Belson. ''I'll clean up here and be along.''

As we started out I said to Belson, ''I'm still double-parked out there. Let me get it off the street before some zealous meter maid gets it hauled off.''

Belson said, ''Why don't you follow me downtown. Then we won't have to drive you back later.''

I nodded and grinned. ''See? I told you you didn't think I did it.''

''I don't think anything,'' Belson said. ''But you'll be down to look out for the little girl.''

Belson took Terry into the squad car and they drove off. I got my car out from behind another white and blue police car with the seal of the city on the side, and followed Belson's car up Hemenway to Boylston, down Boylston to Clarendon, right on Clarendon, then up the Stanhope Street Alley and in behind headquarters.

• 5 •

We went in the back door, off Stanhope Street by the parking area that says RESERVED FOR PRESS. There were no cars there. You only go in the front door if you're news-film material. If they put the arm on you in a dis-advantaged neighborhood you go in past the empty press lot.

The Homicide Division was third floor rear, with a view of the Fryalator vent from the coffee shop in the alley and the soft perfume of griddle and grease mixing with the indigenous smell of cigar smoke and sweat and something else, maybe generations of scared people. Vince Haller was leaning against one of the desks outside Quirk's frosted glass cubicle. He was wearing a white double-knit suit, and over one shoulder he carried a camel's-hair coat with big leather buttons. His gray hair was long and modish and he had a big Teddy Roosevelt mustache. He was a couple of inches taller than I was, but not as heavy.

"Gentlemen?" he said in his big actorish voice.

I gave him a wave and Belson said, "Hello, Vince."

"I'd like a chance to talk to my client."

Belson looked at Terry Orchard. "Is this man your attorney?"

She looked at me and I nodded. She said, "Yes."

"You can talk with her at my desk there." Belson nodded at a scarred and cluttered desk outside Quirk's enclosed cubicle. "We'll stay out of earshot."

"Has she been charged, Frank?" Haller asked.

"Not yet."

32

"Will she be?"

"I don't know. The lieutenant will be along in a minute. He takes care of that stuff. We'll want to talk with her a lot, though, either way."

"Has she been advised of her rights?"

Belson snorted. "Are you kidding. If she were shooting at me with a flame thrower I'd have to advise her of her rights before I shot back. Yes, she's been advised."

"Have you, Miss Orchard?"

"Yes, sir." She was numb and scared, and entirely submissive.

"Okay, come over here and we'll talk." She did, and Belson and I stood silently watching them. I suddenly realized how tired I was. I'd slept about three hours. As we stood there, Quirk came in with two other dicks. He looked over at Haller and Terry Orchard, said nothing, and walked into his cubicle. Belson went in after him.

"Stick around," he said. And closed the door. The two dicks sat down at desks, and looked at nothing.

At the other end of the office a black cop with thick hands and a broken nose was talking into a telephone receiver cradled on one shoulder. An old guy in green coveralls came through dragging a cardboard carton with a rope handle and emptying the ashtrays and wastebaskets into it. Haller was still talking to Terry. And I thought about all the times I'd spent in shabby squad rooms like this. Sometimes it felt like all the rooms I was ever in looked out onto alleys. And I thought about how it must feel to be twenty and alone and be in one at 5:30 A.M. and not sure you'd get out. The steam pipes hissed. I wanted to hiss back.

More than that I wanted to run. The room was hot and stuffy. The air was bad. I wanted to get out, to get in my car and drive north. In my mind I could see the route, over the Mystic Bridge up Route One, north, maybe to Ipswich or Newburyport where the houses were stately and old and the air was clean and cold and full of the sea. Where there's a kind of mellowness and a memory of another time and another America. Probably never was another America though. And if I headed out that way I'd probably be sitting around the police station in Ipswich, smelling the steam pipes and the disinfectant and wondering if some poor slob deserved what he was getting.

Quirk came out of his office. And looked at Haller. Then turned to me.

"Come in and talk."

I did. I told the same story to Quirk that I had to Belson. Exactly the same way. Quirk listened without a word. Looking straight at me all the time I talked. When I was through he said, "Okay, wait outside."

I did. He called Terry Orchard in. Haller went with her. The door closed. I sat some more. The dick at the end of the room still talked into the phone. The two that had come in with Quirk continued to sit and look elaborately at nothing. The sun had come up and shone into one corner of the room. Dust motes drifted in languidly.

"I can't stand it anymore," I said. "I'll confess, just don't give me the silent treatment anymore."

The two detectives looked at me blankly. "Confess what?" one of them said. He had long curly sideburns.

"Anything you want, just no more of the cold shoulder."

Sideburns said to his partner, "Hey, Al, ain't he a funny guy? Right before you go off duty after working all night it's really great to have a funny guy like him around so you can go home happy. Don't you feel that way, Al?"

Al said, "Aw, screw him."

More silence. I got up and walked to the window. There was a heavy wire mesh across it so suspects wouldn't jump out, drop three stories to the ground, and run off. The windows were grimy, with a kind of ancient grime that seemed to have sunk into the glass. Three floors below a thin Puerto Rican kid with pointed shoes came out of the back of the coffee shop with a bucket and poured hot dirty water into the street. It steamed in the cold briefly. I looked at my watch, 6:40. The kid had got up awful early to come in and mop the floor. I wondered how late tonight he'd be there.

Belson came out of Quirk's office with Terry, through the squad room, and out. Haller came out too, and walked over to me.

"They've gone down to the lab. I think they'll book her," he said. I didn't say anything.

He said, "Quickly, I wanted to check her story with you. She was asleep with her boy friend in their apartment. Two men apparently known to Powell entered. Shot Powell, forced her to shoot Powell's body, drugged her, and left. She called you. You came. Sobered her up, got her story. Called the cops."

"That's it," I said.

"She knows you because the university employed you to find a missing rare book."

"Manuscript," I said.

"Okay, manuscript . . . You got in touch with her because the campus security man suggested that an organization she was part of might have taken it. She had your card. In trouble she called you."

"Right again," I said.

"As stories go it's not a winner," Haller said.

"I know," I said.

"She's convincing when she tells it, though," said Haller.

"What's its effect on Quirk?" I asked.

"Hard to say. He doesn't show much, but I don't think he's easy about it. I think he'll book her but I don't think he's sure she's guilty."

"What do you think?" I asked.

"All my clients are innocent."

"Yeah," I said, "of something, anyway."

While we waited, the shift changed. Al and Sideburns left. The black cop with the phone had departed. The day people came in. Faces shaved. Wind-reddened. Smelling of cologne. Some of them had coffee in paper cups they'd bought on the way in. It smelled good. No one offered me any. Belson came back into the office with Terry. They went back into Quirk's office. Haller went with them. Quirk yelled from inside.

"Spenser, come in. You might as well hear the rest."

I went in. It was crowded in there. Quirk was behind his desk. Terry in a straight chair beside it. Belson, Haller, and I standing against the wall. Quirk's desk was absolutely bare except for a tape recorder and a transparent plastic cube which on all sides contained pictures of a woman, children, and an English setter.

Quirk turned the recorder on. "All right, Miss Orchard, your story and Spenser's match. But that proves nothing much. You had plenty of time to arrange it before we were called. Can you think of any reason why two men would wish to come and kill Dennis Powell?"

"No, I don't know, maybe." Terry spoke barely above a whisper and she seemed to sway slightly in the chair as she spoke.

"Which is it, Miss Orchard?" Quirk's voice was almost entirely without inflection and his thick pockmarked face was entirely impassive. Terry shook her head.

Haller said, "Really, Lieutenant, Miss Orchard is about to fall from the chair." When Haller talked the orange level light on the recorder flared brightly.

"Which is it, Miss Orchard?" Quirk said again, as if Haller hadn't spoken.

"Well, I think he was involved in the manuscript."

36

"Which manuscript?"

"The one that Mr. Spenser is looking for, the what-chamacallit manuscript."

I said, "Godwulf," and Quirk said, "Is it the Godwulf Manuscript, Miss Orchard?"

She nodded.

Quirk said, "Say yes or no, Miss Orchard; the recorder can't pick up signs."

"Yes," she said.

"How was he involved?"

"I don't know, just that he was, and some faculty member was. I heard him talking on the phone one day."

"What did they say?"

"I can't remember."

"Then why do you think it involved the theft of a manuscript?"

"I just know. You know how you remember having an idea from a conversation but not remember the conversation itself, you know?"

"Why do you think a faculty member is involved, Miss Orchard?"

She shook her head again. "Same reason," she said.

"Do you think one of the men who you say killed Powell was a professor?"

"No."

"Why not?"

"I don't know. They didn't look like professors."

"What did they look like?"

"It's hard to remember. It was so fast. They were both big and had on dark topcoats and hats, regular felt hats, like businessmen wear. The one who shot Dennis had big sideburns, like Prince Albert, you know, along his jaw. He was sort of fat."

"Black or white?"

She looked startled. "White," she said.

"Why would the theft of a manuscript cause two big

white men in hats and topcoats to come to your apartment at two-thirty A.M. and kill Powell and frame you?''

''I don't know.''

''Why—'' Quirk stopped. Tears were running down Terry Orchard's face. She made no sound. She sat still with her eyes closed and the tears coming down her face.

I said, ''Quirk, for crissake . . .''

He nodded, turned to Belson.

''Frank, get a matron and book her.'' Belson took her arm. She stood up.

There was no sign that she heard him, or that she heard anything.

Belson took her out. Haller went with her.

Quirk said, ''So far you're out of it, Spenser. I got nothing to hold you for. But if something does come up I want you to be where I don't have to look for you.''

I got up. ''There are whole days at a time, Lieutenant, that go by without me ever giving a real goddamn about what you want.''

Quirk took my gun out of his desk and handed it to me, butt first. ''Beat it,'' he said.

I put the gun away, went down the stairs, three flights and out the front door. There were no cameramen, no TV trucks. It was cold and the wet snow-rain had frozen into gray lumpy ice. I went around the corner, got in my car, drove home, drank two glasses of milk, and went to bed.

• 6 •

The phone woke me again. I squinted against the brutal bright sunlight and answered.

"Spenser?"

"Yeah."

"Spenser, this is Roland Orchard." He paused as if waiting for applause.

I said, "How nice for you."

He said, "What?"

I said, "What do you want, Mr. Orchard?"

"I want to see you. How soon can you get here?"

"As soon as I feel like it. Which may be a while."

"Spenser, do you know who I am?"

"I guess you're Terry Orchard's father."

He hadn't meant that. "Yes," he said. "I am. I am also senior partner of Orchard, Bonner and Blanch."

"Swell," I said. "I buy all your records."

"Spenser, I don't care for your manner."

"I'm not selling it, Mr. Orchard. You called me. I didn't call you. If you want to tell me what you want without showing me your scrapbook, I'll listen. Otherwise, write me a letter."

There was a long silence. Then Orchard said, "Do you have my address, Mr. Spenser?"

"Yeah."

"My daughter is home, and I have not gone into the office, and we would very much like you to come to the house. I expect to pay you."

"I will come out in about an hour, Mr. Orchard," I said, and hung up.

It was a little after noon. I got up and stood a long time under the shower. I'd had about four and a half hours' sleep and I needed more. Ten years ago I wouldn't have. I put on my suit—I wasn't sure you could get onto West Newton Hill without one—made and ate a fried egg sandwich, drank a cup of coffee, and went out. I should have made the bed. I knew I would hate finding it unmade when I came back.

It was cold and bright out. It took five minutes for the heater in the car to get warm enough to melt the ice on my windows, and another five minutes for it to melt. I had no ice scraper.

By the Mass Turnpike it is less than ten minutes from downtown Boston to West Newton. From West Newton Square to the top of West Newton Hill is a matter of fifty thousand dollars. Status ascends as the hill rises and at the top live the rich. It is old rich on West Newton Hill. Doctor rich, professor rich, stockbroker rich, lawyer rich. The new rich, the engineer rich, and the technocratic rich live in developments named after English kings in towns like Lynnfield and Sudbury.

Roland Orchard looked to be a rich man's rich man. His home was large and white and towering as one came up the hill toward it. It occupied most of the lot it was built on. New rich seem to want a lot of land for a gardener to manicure. Old rich don't seem to give a damn. Across the front and around one side of the house was a wide porch, empty in the winter but bearing the wear marks of summer furniture. Above the door was a fan-shaped stained glass window. I rang the bell. A maid opened the door. Her black skin, devoid of make-up, shone as though freshly burnished. Her almond-colored eyes held a knowledge of things that West Newton Hill didn't want to hear about.

She said, "Yes, sir."

I gave her one of my cards. The one with only my name on it.

"Yes, Mr. Spenser. Mrs. Orchard is expecting you in the study."

She led me down a polished oak-floored hall, past a curving stairway. The hall—it was more like a corridor—ran front to back, the depth of the house. At the far end a floor to ceiling window opened out onto the back yard. The coils of a grapevine framed the window. The rest was dirty snow. The maid knocked on a door to the left of the window; a woman's voice said, "Come in." The maid opened the door, said, "Mr. Spenser," and left.

It was a big room, blond wood bookcases built in on three walls. A fieldstone fireplace covered the fourth wall. There was a fire going and the room was warm and smelled of woodsmoke. Mrs. Orchard was standing when I came in. She was darkly tanned (not Miami, I thought, West Palm Beach probably) and wearing a white pants suit and white boots. Her hair was shag cut and tipped with silver and the skin on her face was very tight over her bones. She had silver nail polish and wore heavy Mexican-looking silver earrings. A silver service and a covered platter on a mahogany tea wagon stood near the fire. A chiffon stole was draped over the back of the couch, and a novel by Joyce Carol Oates lay open on the coffee table.

As I walked toward her, she stood motionless, one hand extended, limp at the wrist, toward me. I felt as if I were walking into a window display.

"Mr. Spenser," she said. "It's very nice of you to come."

"That's okay," I said.

I didn't know what to do with her hand, shake it or kiss it. I shook it, and the way she looked made me suspect I'd chosen wrong.

"My husband had to go into the office for a bit, he should be back soon."

I said, "Uh huh."

"He might have stopped off at the club for handball and a rubdown. Rolly works very hard to stay in shape."

"Uh huh."

"What do you do, Mr. Spenser? You look to be in excellent condition. Do you work out?"

"Not at the club," I said.

"No," she said. "Of course not."

I took off my coat. "May I sit down?" I said.

"Oh, I'm sorry, of course, sit down. Will you have some coffee, or tea? I had some sandwiches made up. Would you like one?"

"No, thank you, I ate before I came. I'll take coffee though, black."

"You must pardon me, Mr. Spenser, my manners are really much better. It's just that I've never been involved with policemen and all. And I have never really spoken to a private detective before. Are you carrying a gun?"

"I thought I'd risk West Newton without one," I said.

"Yes, of course. You're sure you won't have a sandwich?"

"Look, Mrs. Orchard, I spent most of last night with your daughter and a corpse. I spent the rest of last night with your daughter and the cops. The last I knew she was in jail for murder. Your husband says she's home. Now he and you didn't get me out here to make sure I was eating properly. What do you want?"

"My husband will be along soon, Mr. Spenser; he'll explain. Rolly handles these thing. I do not." She looked straight at me as she talked and leaned a little forward. She had large blue eyes, and she wore eye shadow, I noticed. I bet the eyes got her a lot that she wanted. Especially when she looked right at you and leaned a little forward as she talked. She turned a little on the couch and tucked one leg

42

under the other, and I got the long line of her thigh and the jut of her sharp breasts. Her body looked lean and tight. A little sinewy for my taste. She kept the pose. I wondered if I was supposed to bark.

She picked up the book. "Do you read much, Mr. Spenser?"

"Yeah," I said.

"Do you enjoy Miss Oates?"

"No."

"Oh, really? Why on earth not?"

"I'm probably insensitive," I said.

"Oh, I don't think so, Mr. Spenser. What little I've heard Terry say of you suggests quite the contrary."

"Where is Terry?"

"In her room. Her father has asked that she talk with no one except in his presence."

"How's she feel about that?"

"After what she's gotten herself into and what she's putting us through, she's learning to do what she's told."

There was a triumphant undertone in Mrs. Orchard's voice. I said nothing.

"Would you put another log on the fire, Mr. Spenser? It seems to be going low, and Rolly always likes a blazing fire when he comes in."

It was a way of establishing relationships, I thought, as I got a log from the basket and set it on top of the fire—get me to do her bidding. I'd known other women like that. If they couldn't get you to do them little services they felt insecure. Or, maybe she just wanted another log on the fireplace. Sometimes I'm deep as hell.

The door to the study opened and a man came in. He wore a dark double-breasted blazer with a crest on the pocket, a thick white turtleneck sweater, gray flared slacks, and black ankle boots with a lot of strap and buckle showing. His hair was blond and no doubt naturally curly; it contrasted nicely with his tan. He was a slender man, shorter than I by maybe an inch and maybe ten years older. Under the tan his face had a reddish flush which might be health or booze.

"Spenser," he said and put out his hand, "kind of you to come." I shook hands with him. He wasn't being the top-exec-used-to-instant-obedience. He was being the gracious-man-of-affluence-putting-an-employee-at-ease.

He said to his wife, "I'll have coffee, Marion."

She rose and poured him coffee. She put several small triangular sandwiches on a plate, put the coffee cup in the little depression on the plate that was made to hold it, and placed it next to a red leather wing chair.

Orchard sat down, carefully hiking his trouser legs up at the knee so they wouldn't bag. I noticed he had a thick silver ring on his little finger.

"I'm sorry to have kept you waiting, Spenser, but I don't like to stay out of work if I can help it. Married to the job, I guess. Just wanted to make sure everything was running smoothly."

He took a delicate sip of coffee and a small bite of one of the sandwiches.

"I wish to hire you, Mr. Spenser, to see that my daughter is exonerated of the charges leveled against her. I was able to have her released on bail in my custody, but it took a good deal of doing and I had to collect a number of favors to do it. Now I want this mess cleared up and the suspicion eliminated from my name and my home. The police are working to convict. I want someone working to acquit."

"Why not have Terry join us?" I said.

"Perhaps later," Orchard said, "but first I want to speak with you for a time."

I nodded. He went on. "I would like you to give me a complete rundown of the circumstances by which you became involved with Terry up to and including last night."

"Hasn't Terry told you?"

"I want your version."

I didn't want to tell him. I didn't like him. I did like his daughter. I didn't like his assumption that our versions would differ. I said, "Nope."

"Mr. Spenser. I am employing you to investigate a murder. I want a report of what you've discovered so far."

"First, you may or may not be hiring me. You've offered. I haven't accepted. So at the moment I owe you nothing. That includes how I met your daughter, and what we did."

"Goddammit, Spenser, I don't have to take that kind of insolence from you."

"Right," I said, "you can hire another Hawkshaw. The ones with phones are in the yellow pages under SLEUTH."

I thought for a moment that Orchard was going to get up and take a swing at me. I felt no cold surge of terror. Then he thought better of it, and leaned back in his chair.

"Marion," he said, "I'll have some brandy. Would you join me, Mr. Spenser?" I looked at my watch; it was 2:30. He really handled stress well. I decided what the flush under the tan was.

"Yeah. I'll have some. Thank you."

Marion Orchard's face looked a little more tightly stretched over her good bones as she went to the sideboard and poured two shots of brandy from a decanter into crystal snifters. She brought them back to us, handed one to me and one to her husband.

Orchard swirled it in his glass and took a large swallow. I tried mine. It was the real stuff okay, barely liquid at all as it drifted down my throat. A guy who served brandy like that couldn't be all bad.

"Now look, Spenser. Terry is our only child. We've lavished every affection and concern on her. We have

45

brought her up in wealth and comfort. Clothes, the best schooling, Europe. She had her own horse and rode beautifully. She made us proud. She was an achiever. That's important. We do things in this family. Marion rides and hunts as well as any man.''

I looked at Marion Orchard and said, ''Hi ho, Silver.'' Orchard went on. I was not sure he'd heard me.

''Then when it came time for college, she insisted on going to that factory. Can you imagine the reaction of some of my associates when they ask me where my daughter goes to school and I tell them?'' It was a rhetorical question. I could imagine, but I knew he wasn't looking for an answer. ''Against my best judgment I permitted her to go. And I permitted her to live there rather than at home.'' He shook his head. ''I should have known better. She got in with the worst element in a bad school and . . .'' He stopped, drank another large slug from his snifter, and went on. ''She never gave us any trouble till then. She was just what we wanted. And then in college, living on the very edge of the ghetto, sleeping around, drugs. You've seen her, you've seen how she dresses, who she keeps company with. I don't even know where she lives anymore. She rarely comes home and when she does it's as if she were coming only to flaunt herself before us and our friends. Do you know she appeared here at a party we were giving wearing a miniskirt she'd made out of an old pair of Levis? Now she's gotten herself involved in a murder. I've got a right to know about her. I've got a right to know what she'll do to us next.''

''I don't do family counseling, Mr. Orchard. There are people who do and maybe you ought to look up one of them. If you'll get Terry down here we'll talk, all of us, and see if we can arrange to live in peace while I look into the murder.''

Orchard had finished his brandy. He nodded at the empty glass. His wife got up, refilled it, and brought it to him. He drank, put the glass down. He said, "While you're up, Marion, would you ask Terry to come down."

Marion left the room. Orchard took another belt of brandy. He wasn't bothering to savor the bouquet. I nibbled at the edge of mine. Marion Orchard came back into the room with Terry.

I stood and said, "Hello, Terry."

She said, "Hi."

Her hair was loose and long. She wore a short-sleeved blouse, a skirt, no socks, and a pair of loafers. I looked at her arms, no tracks. One point for our side; she wasn't shooting. At least not regularly. She was fresh-scrubbed and pale, and remarkably without affect. She went to a round leather hassock by the fire and sat down, her knees tight together, her hands folded in her lap. Dolly Demure, with a completely blank face. The loose hair softened her, and the traditional dress made her look like somebody's cheerleader, right down to loafers without socks. Had there been any animation she's have been pretty as hell.

Orchard spoke. "Terry, I'm employing Mr. Spenser to clear you of the murder charge."

She said, "Okay."

"I hope you'll cooperate with him in every way."

"Okay."

"And, Terry, if Mr. Spenser succeeds in getting you out of this mess, *if* he does, perhaps you will begin to rethink your whole approach to life."

"Why don't you get laid," she said flatly, without inflection, and without looking at him.

Marion Orchard said, "Terry," in a horrified voice.

Orchard's glass was empty. He flicked an eye at it, and away.

"Now you listen to me, young lady," he said. "I have put up with your nonsense for as long as I'm going to. If you . . ."

I interrupted. "If I want to listen to this kind of crap I

47

can go home and watch daytime television. I want to talk with Terry, and maybe later I'll want to talk with each of you. Separately. Obviously I was wrong; we can't do it in a group. You people want to encounter one another, do it on your own time."

"By God, Spenser," Orchard said.

I cut him off again. "I want to talk with Terry. Do I or don't I?"

I did. He and his wife left, and Terry and I were alone in the library.

"If I told my father to get laid he would have knocked out six of my teeth," I said.

"Mine won't," she said. "He'll drink some more brandy, and tomorrow he'll stay late at the office."

"You don't like him much," I said.

"I bet if I said that to you, you'd knock out six of my teeth," she said.

"Only if you didn't smile," I answered.

"He's a jerk."

"Maybe," I said. "But he's your jerk, and from his point of view you're no prize package either."

"I know," she said.

"However," I said, "let's think about what I'm supposed to do here. Tell me more about the manuscript and the professor and anything else you can remember beyond what you told Quirk last night."

"That's all there is," she said. "I told the police everything I know."

"Let's run through it again anyway," I said. "Have you talked with Quirk again since last night?"

"Yes, I saw him this morning before Daddy's people got me out."

"Okay, tell me what he asked you and what you said."

"He started by asking me why I thought two big white men in hats would come to our apartment and kill Dennis and frame me."

48

That was Quirk, starting right where he left off, no rephrasing, no new approach, less sleep than I had and there in the morning when the big cheeses passed the word along to let her out, getting all his questions answered before he released her.

"And what did you answer?" I said.

"I said the only thing I could think of was the manuscript. That Dennis was involved somehow in that theft and he was upset about it."

"Can you give me more than that? How was he involved? Why was he involved? What makes you think he was involved? Why do you think he was upset? What did he do to show you he was upset? Answer any or all, one at a time."

"It was a phone call he made from the apartment. The way he was talking I could tell he was upset and I could tell he wasn't talking to another kid. I mean you can tell that from the way people talk. The way his voice sounded."

"What did he say?" I said.

"I couldn't hear most of it. He talked low, and I knew he didn't want me to hear, you know, cupping his hand and everything. So I tried not to hear. But he did say something about hiding it . . . like 'Don't worry, no one will find it. I was careful.' "

"When was this?" I asked.

"About a week ago. Lemme see, I was up early for my Chaucer course, so it would have been Monday, that's five days ago. Last Monday."

The manuscript had been stolen Sunday night.

"Okay, so he was upset. About what?"

"I don't know, but I can tell when he's mad. At one point I think he threatened someone."

"Why do you think so? What did he say that makes you think so?"

"He said, 'If you don't . . .' No . . . No . . . he said, 'I will, I really will . . .' Yeah. That's what it was . . . 'I really will.' But very threateny, you know.''

"Good. Now why do you think it was a professor? I know the voice tone told you it was someone older, but why a professor? What did he say? What were the words?''

"Well, oh I don't know, it was just a feeling. I wasn't all that interested; I was running the water for a bath anyway.''

"No, Terry, I want to know. The words, what were his words?''

She was silent, her eyes squeezed almost shut as if the sun were shining in them, her upper teeth exposed, her lower lip sucked in.

"Dennis said, 'I don't care' . . . 'I don't care, if you do' . . . He said, 'I don't care if you do. Cut the goddamn thing.' That's it. He was talking to an older person and he said cut the class if the other person had to. That's why I figured it must be a professor.''

"How do you know he wasn't talking about cutting a piece of rope, or a salami?''

"Because he mentioned class or school a little before. And what could they be talking about angrily that had to do with salami?''

"Okay. Good. What else?''

There wasn't anything else. I worked on her for maybe half an hour more and nothing else surfaced. All I got was the name of a SCACE official close to Powell, someone named Mark Tabor, whose title was political counselor.

"If you think of anything else, anything at all, call me. You still have my card?''

"Yes. I . . . my father will pay you for what you did last night.''

"No, he won't. He'll pay me for what I may do. But last night was a free introductory offer.''

"It was a very nice thing to do,'' she said.

"Aw, hell,'' I said.

"What you should try to do is this," I said. "You should try to keep from starting up with your old man for a while. And you should try to stay around the house, go to class if you think you should, but for the moment let SCACE stave off the apocalypse without you. Okay?"

"Okay. But don't laugh at us. We're perfectly serious and perfectly right."

"Yeah, so is everyone I know."

I left her then. Said good-bye to her parents, took a retainer from Roland Orchard, and drove back to town.

Driving back to Boston, I thought about my two retainers in the same week. Maybe I'd buy a yacht. On the other hand maybe it would be better to get the tear in my convertible roof fixed. The tape leaked. I got off the Mass Pike at Storrow Drive and headed for the university. On my left the Charles River was thick and gray between Boston and Cambridge. A single oarsman was sculling upstream. He had on a hooded orange sweat shirt and dark blue sweat pants and his breath steamed as he rocked back and forth at the oars. Rowing downstream would have been easier.

I turned off Storrow at Charlesgate, went up over Commonwealth, onto Park Drive, past a batch of ducks swimming in the muddy river, through the Fenway to Westland Ave. Number 177 was on the left, halfway to Mass Ave. I parked at a hydrant and went up the stone steps to the glass door at the entry. I tried it. It was open. Inside an ancient panel of doorbells and call boxes covered the left wall. I didn't have to try one to know they didn't work. They didn't need to. The inner door didn't close all the way because the floor was warped in front of the sill and the door jammed against it. Mark Tabor was on the fourth floor. No elevator. I walked up. The apartment house smelled bad and the stair landing had beer bottles and candy wrappers accumulating in the corners. Somewhere in the building electronic music was playing at top volume. The fourth flight began to tell on me a little but I forced myself to breathe normally as I knocked on Tabor's door. No anwer. I knocked again. And a third time. Loud. I didn't want to waste the four-flight climb. A voice inside called out, "Wait a minute." There was a pause and then the door opened.

I said, "Mark Tabor?"

And he said, "Yeah."

He looked like a zinnia. Tall and thin with an enormous corona of rust red hair flaring out around his pale, clean-shaven face. He wore a lavender undershirt and a pair of faded, flare-bottomed denim dungarees that were too long and dragged on the floor over his bare feet.

I said, "I'm a friend of Terry Orchard's; she asked me to come and talk with you."

"About what?"

"About inviting people in to sit down."

"Why do you think I know what's her name?"

"Aw, come off it, Tabor," I said. "How the hell do you think I got your name and address? How do you know Terry Orchard is not a what's *his* name? What do you lose by talking with me for fifteen minutes? If I was going to mug you I would have already. Besides, a mugger would starve to death in this neighborhood."

"Well, what do you want to talk about?" he asked, still standing in the door. I walked past him into the room. He said, "Hey," but didn't try to stop me. I moved a pile of mimeographed pamphlets off a steamer trunk and sat down on it. Tabor took a limp pack of Kools out of his pants pocket, extracted a ragged cigarette, and lit it. The menthol smell did nothing for the atmosphere. He took a big drag and exhaled through his nose. He leaned against the door jamb. "Okay," he said. "What do you want?"

"I want to keep Terry Orchard out of the slam, for one thing. And I want to find the Godwulf Manuscript for another."

"Why are the cops hassling Terry?"

"Because they think she killed Dennis Powell."

"Dennis is dead?"

I nodded.

"Ain't that a bitch, now," he said, much as if I'd said the rain would spoil the picnic. He went over and sat on the edge of a kitchen table covered with books, lined yellow paper, manila folders, and the crusts of a pizza still in the take box. Behind him, taped to the gray painted wall with raggedly torn masking tape, was a huge picture of Che Guevara. Opposite was a day bed covered by an unzipped sleeping bag. There were clothes littered on the floor. On top of a bureau was a hot plate. There were no curtains nor window shades.

I clucked approvingly. "You've really got some style, Tabor," I said.

"You from *House Beautiful* or something?" he said.

"Nope, I'm a private detective." I showed him the photostat of my license. "I'm trying to clear Terry Orchard of the murder charge. I'm also looking for the Godwulf Manuscript and I think they're connected. Can you help me?"

"I don't know nothing about no murder, man, and nothing about no jive ass manuscript." Why did all the radical white kids from places like Scarsdale and Bel Air try to talk as if they'd been brought up in Brownsville and Watts? He stubbed out his Kool and lit another.

"Look," I said. "You and Dennis Powell roomed together for two years. You and Terry Orchard are members of the same organization. You share the same goals. I'm not the cops. I'm free-lance, for crissake, I'm labor. I work for Terry. I don't want you. I want Terry out of trouble and the manuscript back in its case. Do you know where the manuscript is?"

"Naw, man. I don't know anything about it."

He didn't look up from the contemplation of his Kool. His voice never varied. Like Terry, he showed no affect. No response to stimulus. It was as though he'd shut down.

"Tell me this," I said. "Does SCACE have a faculty adviser?"

"Oh, man, be cool. SCACE ain't no frat house, baby. Faculty adviser . . . Man, that's heavy."

"Do any faculty members belong to SCACE?"

"Maybe. Lot of people belong to SCACE. That's for me to know and you to guess."

"What's the big secret?"

"Lots of dudes can get in trouble for joining organizations like SCACE. The imperialists don't like opposition. The fat cats don't like organizations that are for the worker. The superoppressors are scared of the revolution."

"You forgot to mention the capitalist running dog lackies," I said.

"Like you, you mean? See what happened to Terry Orchard? The pigs have framed her already. They'll do anything they can to stamp us out."

"Look, kid. I don't want to sit up here and argue Herbert Marcuse with you. The cops are professionals. You can sit here in your hippie suit and drink wine and smoke grass and read Marx and play revolution like Tom Sawyer ambushing the A-rabs all you want. That bothers the cops like a tick fly on an elephant. If they wanted to stamp you out they'd come in here and stamp and you'd know what a stamping was. They don't have to get frilly and frame some twenty-year-old broad to get at you. They've got guys in the station house in Charlestown that they keep in a cage when they're not on duty."

He gave me a tough look. Which isn't easy when you weigh 150 pounds.

"How about a faculty member that might be associated with SCACE?"

He let the smoke from his cigarette out of his nose and mouth slowly. It drifted up around his head. Long years of practice, I thought. He looked straight at me with his eyes almost closed for a long time. Then he said, "Where would the movement be now if someone had saved Sacco and Vanzetti?"

"Sonova bitch," I said. "You're almost perfect, you are, a flawless moron. I don't think I've ever seen anyone stay so implacably on the level of absolute abstraction."

"Screw you, man," he said.

"That's better," I said. "Now we're getting down where I live. I've got no hope for you, punk. But I promise you that if that kid gets burned because you don't tell me what you could tell me, I will come for you. You martyr that kid and I'll give the movement another martyr."

"Screw you, man," he said.

I walked out.

I went back down the four flights of stairs, as empty as when I went up. Some sleuth, Spenser, a real Hawkshaw. All you've found out is you get winded after four flights of stairs. I wondered if I should go back up and have a go at shaking some information out of him. Maybe later. Maybe he'd stew a little and I could call on him again. I didn't even know he knew anything. But talking to him, I could feel him holding back. I could feel even that he liked knowing something and not telling. It added color to the romance of his conspiracy. Out in the street the air was cold and it tasted clean after the mentholated smoke and the stale air of Tabor's room. A truck backfired and up on Mass Avenue a bus ground under way in low gear.

My next try was the campus. The student newspaper was located in the basement of the library. On the blond oak door cut into the cinder block of the basement corridor an inventive person had lettered NEWS in black ink.

Inside, the room was long and narrow. L-shaped black metal desks with white Formica tops were sloppily lined up along the long wall on the left. A hand-lettered sign made from half a manila folder instructed the staff to label all photographs with name, date, and location. The room was empty except for a black woman in a red paisley dashiki and matching turban. She was fat but not flabby, hard fat we used to call it when I was a kid, and the dashiki billowed around her body like a drop cloth on the sofa when the living room's going to be painted. A plastic name plate on her desk said FEATURE EDITOR.

She said, "Can I help you?" Her voice was not cordial. No one seemed to be mistaking me for a member of the academic community.

I said, "I hope so."

I gave her a card. "I'm working on a case, and I'm looking for information. Can I ask you for some?"

"You surely can," she said. "All the news that's fit to print, that's us."

"Okay, you know there's a manuscript been stolen."

"Yep."

"I have some reason to believe that a radical student organization, SCACE, is involved in the theft."

"Uh huh."

"What I'm looking for are faculty connections with SCACE. What can you tell me?"

"Why you want to know about faculty connections?"

"I have reason to believe that a faculty member was involved in the theft."

"I have reason to believe that information is a two-way go, sweetie," she said. "Ah is a member ob de press, baby. Information is mah business."

I liked her. She was old for a student, maybe twenty-eight. And she was tough.

"Fair enough," I said. "If you'll drop the Stepin Fetchit act, I'll tell you what I can. In trade?"

"Right on, brother," she said.

"Two things. One, what's your name?"

"Iris Milford."

"Two, do you know Terry Orchard?"

She nodded.

"Then you know she's a SCACE member. You also

57

may know she's been arrested for murder." She nodded again.

"I think the manucript theft and the murder are connected." I told her about Terry, and the murder, and Terry's memory of the phone call.

"Someone set her up," I said. "If someone wanted her out of the way they'd just have killed her. They wanted to kill Powell. They wouldn't go to the trouble and take the risk just to frame her. And they wanted to kill Powell in such a way as to keep people from digging into it. And it looked good—a couple of freaky kids living in what my aunt used to call sin. On drugs, long-haired, barefooted, radical, and on a bad trip, one shoots the other and tells some weird hallucinogenic story about guys in trench coats. The Hearst papers would have them part of an international sex club by the second day's story."

"How come you're messing it up, then? If it's so good. How come you don't believe it?"

"I talked to her right after it happened. She's not that good a liar."

"Why ain't it a trip? Maybe she really thinks she's telling you true. you ever been on a trip?"

"No. You?"

"Baby, I'm fat, black, widowed, pushing thirty, and got four kids. I don't need no additional problems. But she could think it happened. Got any better reason for thinking she's not guilty?"

"I like her."

"All right," she said. "That's cool."

"So, what do you know?"

"Not a hell of a lot. The kid Powell was a jerk, sulky, foolish. On a ego trip. Terry, I don't now. I've been in classes with her. She's bright, but she's screwed up. Jesus, they're so miserable, those kids, always so goddamn unhappy about racism and sexism and im-

58

perialism and militarism and capitalism. Man, I grew up in a tarpaper house in Fayette, Mississippi, with ten other kids. We were trying to stay alive; we didn't have time to be that goddamn unhappy.''

"How about a professor?"

"In SCACE, you got me. I do know that there's a lot of talk about drug dealing connected with SCACE."

"For instance?"

"For instance that Powell was dealing, and had big connections. He could get you smack, anything you wanted. But especially smack. A kid that can get unlimited smack is heavy in some circles."

"Mob connection?"

"I don't know. I don't even know whether he really could get a big supply of smack. I just tell you what I hear. Kids like to talk big especially to me because I live in Roxbury, and they figure all us darkies are into drugs and crime, 'cause we been oppressed by you honkie slumlords."

"I want a professor," I said. "Try this. Name me the most radical faculty members in the university."

"Oh, man, how the hell do I know? There's about thirty-five thousand people in this place."

"Name me anyone, any that you know. I'm not the Feds. I'm not going to harass them. They can advocate cannibalism for all I care. I only want to get one kid out of trouble. Make me a list of any you can think of. They don't have to be active. Who is there that might be involved in stealing a manuscript and holding it for ransom?"

"I'll think on it," she said.

"Think on it a lot. Get any of your friends who will think on it too. Students know things that deans and chairmen don't know."

"Ain't that the truth."

"How about an English professor? Wouldn't that be the

59

best bet? It was a medieval manuscript. It was important because it referred to some medieval writer. Wouldn't an English professor be most likely to think of holding it for ransom?''

"Who's the writer it mentions?'' she asked.

"Richard Rolle.''

"How much they want for him?''

"A hundred thousand dollars.''

"I'd give them some dough if they'd promise not to return it. You ever read his stuff?''

I shook my head.

"Don't,'' she said.

"Can you think of any English professors who might fit my bill?''

"There's a lot of flakes in that department. There's a lot of flakes in most departments, if you really want to know. But English . . .'' She whistled, raised her eyebrows, and looked at the ceiling.

"Okay, but who is the flakiest? Who would you bet on if you had to bet?''

"Hayden,'' she said. "Lowell Hayden. He's one of those little pale guys with long limp blond hair that looks like he hasn't started to shave yet, but he's like thirty-nine. You know? Serious as a bastard. Taught a freshman English course two years ago called The Rhetoric of Revolution. You dig? Yeah, he'd be the one, old Dr. Hayden.''

"What's he teach besides freshman English?''

"I don't know for sure. I know he teaches Chaucer, 'cause I took Chaucer with him.'' I felt a little click in the back of my head. Something nudged at me. A Chaucer class had been mentioned before. I tucked the inkling away. I knew I could dredge it up later when I had time. I always could.

"Mrs. Milford, thank you. If you come up with anything, my number's on the card. I have an answering service. If I'm not there leave a message."

"Okay."

I got up and looked around the basement room. "Freedom of the press is a flaming sword," I said. "Use it wisely, hold it high, guard it well."

Iris Milford looked at me strangely. I left.

The corridor in the basement of the library was almost empty. I looked at my watch, 5:05. Too late to find anyone in the English Department. I went home.

In my kitchen I sat at the counter and opened a can of beer. It was very quiet. I turned on the radio. Maybe I should buy a dog, I thought. He'd be glad to see me when I came home. The beer was good. I finished the can. And opened another. Where was I? I ran over the last couple of days in my mind. One, Terry Orchard didn't kill Dennis Powell. That was a working hypothesis. Two, the missing manuscript and the murder were two parts of the same thing and if I found out anything about one, I'd know something about the other. That was another working hypothesis. What did I have in support of these hypotheses? About half a can of beer. There was that click I had when I talked with Iris Milford. Chaucer. She'd had a Chaucer course with Lowell Hayden. I drank the rest of the beer and opened another can. It came back. Terry was up early for her Chaucer course the day Dennis had been telling some professor on the phone to cut his class. I looked at my face reflected in the window over the sink. "You've still got all the moves, kid," I said. But what did it give me? Nothing much, just a little coincidence. But it was something. It suggested some kind of connection. Coincidences are suspect. Old Lowell Hayden looked better to me all the time. I got another beer. After three or four beers everything began looking better to me.

I got a pound of fresh scallops out of the refrigerator and

began to make something called Scallops Jacques for supper. It was a recipe in a French cookbook that I'd gotten for a birthday present from a woman I know. I like to cook and drink while I'm doing it. Scallops Jacques is a complicated affair with cream and wine and lemon juice and shallots and by the time it was done I was feeling quite pleasant. I made some hot biscuits for myself, too, and ate the scallops and biscuits with a bottle of Pouilly Fuissé, sitting at the counter. Afterward I went to bed. I slept heavy and for a long time.

• 8 •

I slept late and woke up feeling very good, though my mouth tasted funny. I went over the the Boston Y.M.C.A. and worked out in the weight room. I hit the light bag and the heavy bag, ran three miles around their indoor track, took a shower, and went down to my office. I was glistening with health and vigor till I got there. You never felt really glistening in my office. It was on Stuart Street, second floor front, half a block down from Tremont. One room with a desk, a file cabinet, and two chairs in case Mrs. Onassis came with her husband. The old iron radiator had no real control and the room, closed for three days, reeked with heat. I stepped over the three-day pile of mail on the floor under the mail slot and went to open the window. It took some effort. I took off my coat, picked up the mail, and sat at my desk to read it. I'd come down mainly to check my mail and the trip had been hardly worth it. There was a phone bill, a light bill, an overdue notice from the Boston Public Library, a correspondence course offering to teach me karate at home in my spare time, a letter from a former client insisting that while I had found his wife she had left again and hence he would not pay my bill, an invitation to join a vacation club, an invitation to buy a set of socket wrenches, an invitation to join an automobile club, an invitation to subscribe to five magazines of my choice at once-in-a-lifetime savings, an invitation to shop the specials on pork at my local supermarket, and a number of less important letters. Nothing from Germaine Greer or Lenny Bernstein, no dinner invitations, no post cards from the Costa del Sol, no mash notes from Helen Gurley Brown. Last week had been much the same.

I stood up and looked out my window. It was a bright day, but cold, and the whores had emerged, working the Combat Zone, looking cold and bizarre in their miniskirts boots and blond wigs. Being seductive at twenty degrees was heavy going, I thought. Being horny at twenty degrees wasn't all that easy either. Things were slow for the whores. It was lunch time and the businessmen were beginning to drift down from Boylston and Tremont and Back Bay offices to have lunch at Jake Wirth's or upstairs in the Athens Olympia. The whores eyed them speculatively, occasionally approached one and were brushed off. The businessmen didn't like to look at them and hurried off in embarrassment when approached, visions of the day's first bloody mary dancing in their heads.

I closed the window, threw most of the mail away, locked the office, and headed for my car. The drive to the university was easy from my office, and I was there in ten minutes. I parked in a slot that said RESERVED FOR UNIVERSITY PRESIDENT and found my way to Tower's office. The secretary was wearing a pink jumpsuit this day. I revised my opinion about her thighs. They weren't too heavy; they were exactly the right size for the jumpsuit. I said, "My name's Spenser. To see Mr. Tower." She said, "Yes, Mr. Spenser, he'll be through in a minute," and went back to her typing. Twice I caught her looking at me while she pretended to check the clock. You haven't lost a thing, kid, I thought. Two campus cops, in uniform, looking unhappy, came out of Tower's office. Tower came to the door with them.

"This is not Dodge City," he said, "you are not goddamn towntamers—" and shut the outer office door behind them as they left. "Dumb bastards," he said. "Come on in, Spenser."

"I'll see you again on the way out," I said to the secretary. She didn't smile.

"What have you got, Spenser?" Tower asked when we were in and sitting.

"A bad murder, some funny feelings, damn little information, some questions, and no manuscript. I think your secretary is hot for me."

Tower's face squeezed down. "Murder?"

"Yeah, the Powell killing. You know about it as well as I do."

"Yeah, bad. I know, sorry you had to get dragged into it. But we're after a manuscript. We're not worried about the murder. That's Lieutenant Quirk's department. He's good at it."

"Wrong. It's my department, too. I think the manuscript and the murder are connected."

"Why?"

"Terry Orchard told me."

"What?" Tower wasn't liking the way the talk was going.

"Terry remembers a conversation on the phone between Dennis Powell and a professor in which Dennis reassured the professor that he'd hidden 'it' well."

"Oh, for crissake, Spenser. The kid's a goddamn junkie. She remembers anything she feels like remembering. You don't buy that barrel of crap she fed you about mysterious strangers and being forced to shoot Dennis, and being drugged and being innocent. Of course she thinks the university's involved. She thinks the university causes famine."

"She didn't say the university. She said a professor."

"She'll say anything. They all will. She knows you're investigating the manuscript and she wants you to get her

65

out of what she's gotten herself into. So she plays little girl lost with you, and you go panting after her like a Saint Bernard dog. Spenser to the rescue. Balls.''

"Tell me about Lowell Hayden," I said.

Tower liked the conversation even less. "Why? Who the hell is employing who? I want to know your results and you start asking me questions about professors.''

"Whom,'' I said.

"What?''

"It's whom, who is employing whom? Or is it? Maybe it's a predicate nominative, in which case . . .''

"Will you come off it, Spenser. I got things to do.''

"Me, too,'' I said. "One of them is to find out about Lowell Hayden. His name has come up a couple of times. He's a known radical. I have it on some authority that he's the most radical on campus. I have it on authority that Powell was pushing heavy drugs and he had heavy drug connections. I know Hayden had an early Chaucer class on the morning that Powell was talking to a professor about cutting his early morning class.''

"That adds up to zero. Do you know how many professors in this university have eight o'clock classes every day? Who the hell is your authority? I know what's going on on my campus and no one's pushing heroin. I don't say no one's using it, but it's isolated. There's no big supplier. If there were I'd know.''

"Sure you would,'' I said. "Sure what I've got about professors and Lowell Hayden adds up to zero, or little more. But he is all I've got for either the murder or the theft. Why not let me think about him? Why not have a look at him? If he's clean I won't bother him. He probably is clean. But if he isn't . . .''

"No. Do you have any idea what happens if it gets out that a P.I. in the employ of the university is investigating a member of the university faculty? No you don't.

66

You couldn't.'' He closed his eyes in holy dread. "You stick to looking for the manuscript. Stay away from the faculty.''

"I don't do piecework, Tower. I take hold of one end of the thread and I keep pulling it in till it's all unraveled. You hired me to find out where the manuscript went. You didn't hire me to run errands. The retainer does not include your telling me how to do my job.''

"You'll stay the hell away from Hayden or you'll be off this campus to stay. I got you hired for this job. I can get you canned just as easy.''

"Do that," I said and walked out. When you have two retainers you get smug and feisty. In the quadrangle I asked a boy in a fringed buckskin jacket where the English Department was. He didn't know. I tried a girl in an ankle-length o.d. military overcoat. She didn't know either. On the third try I got it; first floor, Felton Hall, other end of the campus.

Felton Hall was a converted apartment building, warrened with faculty offices. The main office of the English Department was at the end of the first floor foyer. An outer office with a receptionist/typist and a file cabinet. An inner office with another desk and woman and typewriter, secretary in chief or administrative assistant, or some such, and beyond that, at right angles, the office of the chairman. The receptionist looked like a student. I asked to see the chairman, gave her my card, the one with my name and profession, but without the crossed daggers, and sat down in the one straight-backed chair to wait. She gave the card to the woman in the inner office, who did not look like a student and didn't even look one hell of a lot like a woman, and came back studiously uninterested in me.

Somewhere nearby I could hear the rhythm of a mimeograph cranking out somebody's midterm, or a reading list for someone's course in Byzantine nature poetry of the third century. I got the same old feeling in my stomach. The one I got as a little kid sitting outside the principal's office.

The office was done in early dorm. There were a travel poster with a picture of the Yogoslav coast stuck with Scotch tape to the wall above the receptionist's desk, the announcement of a new magazine that would pay contributors in free copies of the magazine, a big campy poster of Buster Keaton in *The General*, and a number of Van Gogh and Gauguin prints apparently cut off a calendar and taped up. it didn't hold a candle to my collection of Ann Sheridan pinups.

The mannish-looking inner office secretary came to her door.

"Mr. Spenser," she said, "Dr. Vogel will see you now."

I walked through her big office, through two glass doors into the chairman's office, which was still bigger. It had apparently once been the dining room of an apartment, which had been divided by a partition so that it seemed almost a round room because of the large bow window that looked out over a recently built slum. In the arch of the bow was a large dark desk. On one wall was a fireplace, the bricks painted a dark red, the hearth clean and cold. There were books all around the office and pen and ink drawings of historical-looking people I didn't recognize. There were a rug on the floor and a chair with arms—Tower had neither.

Dr. Vogel sat behind the desk, slim, medium height, thick curly hair trimmed round, black and gray intermixed, clean-shaven, wearing a black pin-striped double-breasted suit with six buttons, all buttoned, pink shirt with a wide roll collar, a white tie with black and pink stripes, and a diamond ring on the left little finger. Whatever happened to shabby gentility?

"Sit down, Mr. Spenser," he said. I sat. He was

looking at my card, holding it neatly by the corners before his stomach with both hands, the way a man looks at a poker hand.

"I don't believe I've ever met a private detective before," he said without looking up. "What do you want?"

"I'm investigating the theft of the Godwulf Manuscript," I said, "and I have only the slightest of suggestions that a member of your department might be involved."

"My department? I doubt that."

"Everyone always doubts things like that."

"I'm not sure the generalization is valid, Mr. Spenser. There must be circles where theft surprises no one, and they must be circles with which you're more familiar than I. Why don't you move in those circles, and not these?"

"Because the circles you're thinking of don't steal illuminated manuscripts, nor do they ransom them for charity, nor do they murder undergraduates in the process."

"Murder?" He liked that about half as well as Tower had.

"A young man, student at this university, was murdered. Another student, a young woman, was involved and stands accused. I think the two crimes are connected."

"Why?"

"I have some slight evidence, but even if I didn't, two major crimes committed at the same university among people belonging to the same end of the political spectrum, and probably the same organization, is at least an unusual occurrence, isn't it?"

"Of course, but we're on the edge of the ghetto here . . ."

"Nobody involved was a ghetto resident. No one was black. The victim and the accused were upper-middle-class affluent."

"Drugs?"

"Maybe, maybe not. To me it doesn't look like a drug killing."

"How does it look to the police?"

"The police don't belabor the obvious, Dr. Vogel. The most obvious answer is the one they like best. Usually they're right. They don't have time to be subtle. They are very good at juggling five balls, but there are always six in the game and the more they run the farther behind they get."

"Thus you handle the difficult and intricate problems, Mr. Spenser?"

"I handle the problems I choose to; that's why I'm freelance. It gives me the luxury to worry about justice. The cops can't. All they're trying to do is keep that sixth ball in the air."

"A fine figure of speech, Mr. Spenser, and doubtless excellent philosophy, but it has little relevance here. I do not want you snooping about my department, accusing my faculty of theft and murder."

"What you want is not what I'm here to find out. I'll snoop on your department and accuse your faculty of theft and murder as I find necessary. The question we're discussing is whether it's the easy way or the hard way. I wasn't asking your permission."

"By God, Spenser . . ."

"Listen, there's a twenty-year-old girl who is a student in your university, has taken courses from your faculty, under the auspices no doubt of your department, who is now out on bail charged with the murder of her boy friend. I think she did not kill him. If I am right, it is quite important that we find out who did. Now that may not rate with importance up as high as, say, the implications of homosexualiry in Shakespeare's sonnets, or whether he said *solid* or *sullied*, but it is important. I'm not going to shoot up the place. No rubber hose, no iron maiden. I

70

won't even curse loudly. If the student newspaper breaks the news that a private eye is ravaging the English Department, the hell with it. You can argue it's an open campus and sit tight.''

"You don't understand the situation in a university at this point in time. I cannot permit spying. I sympathize with your passion for justice, if that is in fact what it is, but my faculty would not accept your prying. Violation of academic freedom integral to such an investigation, sanctioned even implicitly by the chairman, would jeopardize liberal education in the university beyond any justification. If you persist I will have you removed from this department by the campus police.''

The campus police I had seen looked like they'd need to outnumber me considerably, but I let that go. Guile, I thought, guile before force. I had been thinking that more frequently as I got up toward forty.

"The freedom I'm worried about is not academic, it's twenty and female. If you reconsider, my number's on the card.''

"Good day, Mr. Spenser.''

I got even. I left without saying good-bye.

On the bulletin board in the corridor was a mimeographed list of faculty office numbers. I took it off as I went by and put it in my pocket. The mannish-looking secretary watched me all the way out the front door.

I walked through the warm-for-early-winter sun of midafternoon across the campus back toward the library. In the quadrangle there was a girl in a fatigue jacket selling brown rice and pinto beans from a pushcart with a bright umbrella. Six dogs raced about barking and bowling one another over in their play. A kid in a cowboy hat and a pea jacket hawked copies of a local underground paper in a rhythmic monotone, a limp and wrinkled cigarette hanging from the corner of his mouth.

I went into the reading room of the library, took off my coat, sat down at a table, and took out my list of English professors. It didn't get me far. There was no one named Sacco or Vanzetti; none had a skull and crossbones by his name. Nine of the names were women; the remaining thirty-three were men. Lowell Hayden's name was right there after Gordon and before Herbert. Why him, I thought. I didn't have a goddamn thing on him. Just his name came up twice and he teaches medieval literature. Why not him? Why not Vogel, why not Tower, why not Forbes, or Tabor, or Iris Milford, why not Terry Orchard if you really get objective? Like a Saint Bernard, Tower had said. Woof. Why not go home and go to bed and never get up? Some things you just had to decide.

I got up, put the list back in my pocket, put on my coat, and headed back out across campus, toward the English Department. Hayden's office was listed as fourth floor Felton. I hoped I could slip past Mary Masculine, the supersecretary. I made it. There was an old elevator to the left of the foyer, out of sight of the English office. It was a cage affair, open shaft, enclosed with mesh. The stairs wound up around it. I took it to the fourth floor, feeling exposed as it crept up. Hayden's office was room 405. On the door was a brown plastic plaque that said DR. HAYDEN. The door was half-open and inside I could hear two people talking. One was apparently a student, sitting in a straight chair, back to the door, beside the desk, facing the teacher. I couldn't see Hayden, but I could hear his voice.

"The problem," he was saying in a deep, public voice, "with Kittredge's theory of the marriage cycle is that the order of composition of *The Canterbury Tales* is unclear. We do not, in short, know that 'The Clerk's Tale' precedes that of 'The Wife of Bath,' for instance."

The girl mumbled something I couldn't catch, and Hayden responded.

"No, you are responsible for what you quote. If you didn't agree with Kittredge you shouldn't have cited him."

Again the girl's mumble. Again Hayden: "Yes, if you'd like to write another paper, I'll read it and grade it. If it's better than this one, it will bring your grade up. I'd like to see an outline or at least a thesis statement, though, before you write it. Okay?"

Mumble.

"Okay, thanks for coming by."

The girl got up and walked out. She didn't look pleased. As she got into the elevator, I reached around and knocked on the open door.

"Come in," Hayden said. "What can I do for you?"

It was a tiny office, just room for a desk, chair, file cabinet, bookcase, and teacher. No windows, sheetrock partitions painted green. Hayden himself looked right at home in the office. He was small, with longish blondish hair. Not long enough to be stylish; long enough to look as though he needed a haircut. He had on a light green dress shirt with a faint brown stripe in it, open at the neck, and what looked like Navy surplus dungarees. The shirt was too big for him and the material bagged around his waist. He was wearing gold-rimmed glasses.

I gave him my card and said, "I'm working on a case involving a former student and I was wondering if you could tell me anything."

He looked at my card carefully, then at me.

"Anyone may have a card printed up. Do you have more positive identification?"

I showed him the photostat of my license, complete with my picture. He looked at at very carefully, then handed it back.

"Who is the student?" he said.

"Terry Orchard," I said.

He showed no expression. "I teach a great many students, Mr. —" he glanced down at my card lying on his desk—"Spenser. What class? What year? What semester?"

"Chaucer, this year, this semester."

He reached into a desk drawer and pulled a yellow cardboard-covered grade book. He thumbed through it, stopped, ran his eyes down a list, and said, "Yes, I have Miss Orchard in my Chaucer course."

Looking at the grade book upside down, I could see he had the student's last name and first initial. If he didn't know her name or whether she was in his class or not without looking her up in his grade book, how, looking at the listing ORCHARD, T., did he know it was *Miss* Orchard? Like Tabor, the zinnia head, no one seemed willing to know old Terry.

"Don't you know the names of your students, Dr. Hayden?" I asked, trying to say it neutrally, not as if I were critical. He took it as if it were critical.

"This is a very large university, Mr. Spenser." He had to check the card again to get my name. I hope he remembered Chaucer better. "I have an English survey course of sixty-eight students, for instance. I cannot keep track of the names, much as I try to do so. One of this university's serious problems is the absence of community. I am really able to remember only those students who respond to my efforts to personalize our relationship. Miss Orchard apparently is not one of those." He looked again at the open grade book. "Nor do her grades indicate that she has been unusually interested and attentive."

"How is she doing?" I asked, just to keep it going. I didn't know where I was going. I was fishing and I had to keep the conversation going.

"That is a matter concerning Miss Orchard and myself." Nice conversation primer, Spenser, you really know how to touch the right buttons.

"Sorry," I said. "I didn't mean to pry, but when you think about it, prying is more or less my business."

"Perhaps," Hayden said. "It is not, however, my business, nor is it, quite frankly, a business for which I have much respect."

"I know it's not important like Kittredge's marriage cycle, but it's better than re-enlisting, I suppose."

"I'm quite busy, Mr. Spenser." He didn't have to check this time. A quick study, I thought.

"I appreciate that, Dr. Hayden. Let me be brief. Terry Orchard is accused of the murder of her boy friend, Dennis Powell." No reaction. "I am working to clear her of suspicion. Is there anything you can tell me that would help?"

"No, I'm sorry, there isn't."

"Do you know Dennis Powell?"

"No, I do not. I can check through my grade books, but I don't recall him."

"That's not necessary. The grade book won't tell me anything. There's nothing at all you can think of? About either?"

"Nothing, I'm sorry, but I don't know the people involved."

"Are you aware that the Godwulf Manuscript has been stolen?"

"Yes, I am."

"Do you have any idea what might have happened to it?"

"Mr. Spenser, this is absurd. I assume your interest relates to the fact that I am a medievalist. I am not, however, a thief."

"Well," I said, "thanks anyway." I got up.

"You're welcome. I'm sorry I wasn't more useful." His voice was remarkable. Deep and resonant, it seemed incongruous with his slight frame. "Thanks for coming by."

As I left the office, two students were waiting outside, sitting on the floor, coats and books in a pile beside them. They looked at me curiously as I entered the elevator. As it descended I could hear Hayden's voice booming, "Come in, Mr. Vale. What can I do for you?"

On the ground floor were two campus policemen and they wanted me. I hadn't eluded Mary Masculine after all. She was hovering in the doorway to the English office. One of the cops was big and fat with a thick pockmarked face and an enormous belly. The other was much smaller, a black man with a neat Sugar Ray mustache and a tailored uniform. They weren't wearing guns, but each had a nightstick stuck in his hip pocket. The fat one took my arm above the elbow in what he must have felt was an iron grip.

"Start walking, trooper," he said, barely moving his lips.

I was frustrated, and angry at Lowell Hayden, and at Mary Masculine, and the university. I said, "Let go of my arm or I'll put a dent in your face."

"You and who else?" he said. It broke my tension.

"Snappy," I said. "On your days off could you come over and be my dialogue coach?"

The black cop laughed. The fat one looked puzzled and let go of my arm.

"What do you mean?" he said.

"Never mind, Lloyd," the black cop said. "Come on, Jim, we got to walk you off campus."

I nodded. "Okay, but not arm in arm. I don't go for that kind of stuff."

"Me neither, Jim. We'll just stroll along."

And we did. The fat cop had his nightstick out and tapped it against his leg as we went out of the building and toward the street. His eyes never left me. Alert, I thought, vigilant. When we got to my car the black cop opened the door for me, with a small graceful flourish.

The fat one said, "Don't come back. Next time you show up here you'll be arrested."

"For crissake," I said. "I'm working for the university. Your boss hired me."

"I don't know nothing about that, but we got our orders. Get out, and stay out."

The black cop said, "I don't know, Jim, but I think maybe you been canceled." He closed the door and stepped back. I started the car and pulled away. They still stood there as I drove off, the fat one looking balefully after me, still slapping his nightstick against his leg.

• 10 •

It was getting dark and the commuter traffic was starting to thicken the streets. I drove slowly back to my office, parked my car, and went in.

When I unlocked my office door the first thing I noticed was the smell of cigarette smoke. I hadn't smoked in ten years. I pushed it open hard and went in low with my gun out. There was someone sitting at my desk, and another man standing against the wall. In the half light the tip of his cigarette glowed. Neither of them moved. I backed to the wall and felt for the light switch. I found it, and the room brightened.

The man against the wall laughed, a thin sound, without humor.

"Look at that, Phil. Maybe if we give him money he'll do that again."

The man at my desk said nothing. He was sitting with his feet up, my chair tipped back, his hat still on, his overcoat still buttoned up, though it must have been ninety in there, wearing rose-colored gold-rimmed glasses. He looked at me without expression, a very tall man, narrow, with high shoulders, 6'4" or 5", probably. Behind the glasses one eye was blank and white and turned partly up. Along the right line of his jaw was a purple birthmark maybe two inches wide, running the whole length of the jaw from chin to ear. His hands were folded across his stomach. Big hands, long square thick fingers, the backs prominently veined, the knuckles lumpy. I could tell he

78

was impressed with the gun in my hand. The only thing that would have scared him more would have been if I had threatened to flog him with a dandelion.

"Put that away," he said. "If he was going to push you I wouldn't have let Sonny smoke." His voice was a harsh whisper, as if he had an artificial throat.

Sonny gave me a moon-faced smile. He was thick and round, running to fat, with mutton-chop sideburns that came to the corners of his mouth. His coat was off and his collar open, the tie at half-mast. Sweat soaked big half-moon circles around his armpit, and his face was shiny with it. I put the gun away.

"A man wants to see you," Phil said. I hadn't seen him move since I came in. His voice was entirely without inflection.

"Joe Broz?" I said.

Sonny said, "What makes you think so?"

Phil said, "He knows me."

"Yeah," I said, "you walk around behind Broz."

Phil said, "Let's go," and stood up. Six-five, at least. When he was standing you could see that his right shoulder was higher than his left.

I said, "What if I don't want to?"

Phil just looked at me. Sonny snickered, "What if he don't want to, Phil?"

Phil said, "Let's go."

We went. Outisde, double-parked, was a Lincoln Continental. Sonny drove; Phil sat in back with me.

It had started to snow again, softly, big flakes, and the windshield wipers made the only sound in the car. I looked at the back of Sonny's neck as he drove. The hair was long and stylish and curled out over the collar of his white trench coat. Sonny seemed to be singing soundlessly to himself as he drove. His head bobbed and he beat gentle time on the wheel with one suede-gloved hand. Phil was a silent and motionless shape in the corner of the back seat.

"Either of you guys seen *The Godfather*?" I asked.

Sonny snorted. Phil ignored me.

"Beat up any good candy store owners lately, Sonny?"

"Don't ride me, Peep, you'll find yourself looking up at the snow."

"I'm heavy work, Sonny. College kids are about your upper limit, I think."

"Goddammit," Sonny started, and Phil stopped him.

"Shut up," Phil said in his gear box voice, and we both knew he meant both of us.

"Just having a little snappy conversation, Phil, to pass the time," I said.

Phil just looked at me and the menace was like a physical force. I could feel anxiety pulse up and down the long muscles of my arms and legs. Going to see Joe Broz was not normally a soothing experience anyway. Not many people looked forward to it.

The ride was short. Sonny pulled to a stop in front of a building on the lower end of State Street. Phil and I got out. I stuck my head back in before I closed the back door.

"If a tough meter maid puts the arm on you, Sonny, just scream and I'll come running."

Sonny swore at me and burned rubber away from the curb.

I followed Phil into the building. We took the self-service elevator to the eleventh floor. The corridor was silent and empty, with marble wainscoting and frosted glass doors. At the far end we went through one marked CONTINENTAL CONSULTING CO. Inside was an empty stainless steel and coral vinyl reception room. There is little that is quieter than an office building after hours and this one was no exception. The lights were all on, the receptionist's desk was geometrically neat. On one wall were staggered prints by Maurice Utrillo.

Phil said, "Gimme your gun."

I hesitated. I didn't like his manner, I didn't like his assumption that I'd do what I was told because he'd told me to, and I didn't like his assumption that if he had to he could make me. On the other hand I'd come this far because I was curious. Something bothered Broz enough to have him send his top hand to bring me in. And Sonny looked a lot like one of the two hoods that Terry had described. Also, Phil didn't seem much to care whether I liked his assumptions or not.

I noticed that there was a gun in Phil's hand and it was pointing at an area somewhere between my eyes. I'd never seen him move. I took my gun out of my hip holster and handed it to him, butt first. People were taking it away from me a lot lately. I didn't like that too much either. Phil stowed my gun away in an overcoat pocket, put away his own gun in the other, and stepped to one of the inner doors of the reception room. It was solid, no glass panel. I heard a buzz and the door clicked open. I looked around and spotted the closed-circuit camera up high in one corner of the reception room. Phil pushed the door open and nodded me through it.

The room was bone white. The first thing I saw was my own reflection in the wide black picture window that stretched the width of the opposite wall. My reflection didn't look too agressive. In front of the window was a broad black desk, neat, with a bank of phones on it. The room was carpeted with something thick and expensive, in a dark blue. There were several black leather chairs about. Along the side wall was an ebony bar with blue leather padding. Leaning against it was Joe Broz.

There was something theatrical about Broz, as if always there was a press photographer downstage left, kneeling to shoot a picture with his big Speed Graphic camera. He was a middle-sized man who stood very straight with his chin up as if squeezing every inch of height out of that which God had given him. He had many teeth—a few too many for his mouth—and they were very prominent and white. His hair was slick black, combed straight back from a high forehead and gray at the temples. The sideburns were long and neatly trimmed. His nose was flat and thick with a slight ski-jump quality to the end that hinted at a break somewhere in the past. He wore a white suit, a white vest, a dark blue shirt, and a white tie. There was a gold chain across the vest, and presumably a gold watch tucked in the vest pocket. I would have bet against a Phi Bete key, but little is sure in life. He had one foot hooked on the brass rail of the bar, and a large diamond ring flashed from his little finger as he turned a thick highball glass in his hands.

"Do you always dress in blue and white?" I asked. "Or do you have the office redone to match your clothes every day?"

Broz sipped a little of his drink, put it down on the bar, and swung fully around toward me, both elbows resting on the bar.

"I have been told," he said in a deep voice that had the phony quality you hear in an announcer's voice when he's not on the air, "that you are a wise-ass punk. Apparently my information was correct. So let's get some ground rules. You are here because I sent for you. You will leave when I tell you to. You are of no consequence. You have no class. If you annoy me I will have someone sprinkle roach powder on you. Do you understand that?"

"Yeah," I said. "I think so, but you better give me a drink. I feel faint."

Phil, who had drifted to a couch in the far corner and sprawled awkwardly on it, let out a soft sound that sounded almost like a sigh.

Broz moved to his desk, sat, and nodded at one of the leather chairs. "Sit down. I got things to say. Phil, make him a drink."

"Bourbon," I said, "with water, and some bitters."

Phil made the drink. He moved stiffly and his hands

seemed like distorted work gloves. But they performed the task with a bare economy of motion that was incongruous. I'd have to be sure not to make any mistakes about Phil.

I leaned back in the black chair and took a sip of the bourbon. It was a little more expensive than the private label stuff I bought. There was too much bitters, but I decided not to call Phil on it. We'd probably have other issues. There was a knock on the door. Phil glanced at the monitor set in the wall by the door, opened the door, and let Sonny in. He had his trench coat folded over his arm, and his tie was neatly up. His neck spilled over slightly around his collar. He walked quietly over to a chair near the couch and sat down, holding the trench coat in his lap. Broz paid no attention to him. He stared at me with his yellowish eyes.

"You're working on a case." It wasn't really a question. I wasn't sure Broz ever asked questions.

I nodded.

"I want to hear about it," Broz said.

I shook my head.

Broz got a big curved-stem meerschaum pipe out of a rack on his desk and carefully began to pack it from a thick silver humidor.

"Spenser, this can be easy or hard. I'd just as soon it was easy, but the choice is yours."

"Look," I said, "one reason people employ me is because they want their business private. If I spill what I know every time anybody asks me, I am not likely to flourish."

"Your chances of flourishing are not very big right now, Spenser." Broz had the pipe packed to his satisfaction and spoke through a blue cloud of aromatic smoke. "I know you are looking for the Godwulf Manuscript. I know that you are working for Roland Orchard. What I want to know is what you've got. There's no breach of confidence in that."

"Why do you want to know?"

"Let's say I'm an interested party."

"Let's say more than that. Why be one-way? You tell me what your interest is; I'll think about telling you what I know."

"Spenser, I'm hanging on to my patience. But it's slipping. I don't have to make swaps with you. I get what I ask for."

I didn't say anything.

From his place Sonny said, "Let me have him, Mr. Broz."

"What are you going to do, Sonny," I said, "sweat all over me till I beg for mercy?"

Phil made his little sighing sounds again. Sonny put his trench coat carefully on the arm of the couch and started toward me. I saw Phil look at Broz and saw Broz nod.

"You been crying for this, you sonova bitch," Sonny said.

I stood up. Sonny was probably thirty pounds heavier than I was and a lot of it was muscle. But some of it was fat, and quickness didn't look to be Sonny's strong suit. He swung a big right hand at me. I rolled away from it and hit him in the middle of the face twice with left hooks, getting my shoulder nicely behind both of them, feeling the shock all the way up into my back. Sonny was tough. It rocked him but he didn't go down. He grabbed at my shirtfront with his left hand and clubbed at me with his right. The punch glanced off my shoulder and caught me under the left eye. I broke his grip by bringing my clenched fists up under his forearm, and then drove my right forearm against the side of his jaw. He stumbled back two steps and sat down. But he got up. He was wary now. His hands up, he began to circle me. I turned as he did. He put his head down and lunged at me. I moved aside and tripped him and he sprawled against Broz's desk, knocking over the pipe rack. Broz never blinked. Sonny pushed himself up from the desk like a man doing his last push-up. He turned and came at me again. His nose was bleeding freely and his shirtfront was bloody. I feinted with my left hand at his stomach and then brought it up over his hands and jabbed him three times on that bloody nose, crossed over with a right hand that caught him in the neck below the ear. He went down face first. This time he stayed. He got as far as his hands and knees and stayed, his head hanging, swaying slightly, with the blood dripping on the azure rug.

Broz spoke to Phil. "Get him out of here, he's messing on the rug." Phil got up, walked over, pulled Sonny to his feet by the back of his collar, and walked him, weaving and swaying, out through a side door.

Broz said, "Sonny seems to have exaggerated his ability."

"Maybe he just underestimated mine," I said.

"Either way," Broz said.

Phil came back in, wiping his hands on a handkerchief. "Ask him again, Joe," he rasped, "now that Sonny's got him softened." His face twisted in what was, I think, a momentary smile.

Broz looked disgusted. "I want you out of this business, Spenser."

"Which business?"

"The Godwulf Manuscript. I don't want you muddying up the water."

"What's in it for me if I pull out?"

"Health."

"You gonna unleash Sonny on me again?"

"I can put ten Sonnys on your back whenever I want to. Or Phil. Phil's not Sonny."

"I never though he was," I said. "But I hired on to find the manuscript."

"Maybe the manuscript will turn up." Broz leaned back in the big leather executive swivel with the high back, and blew a lungful of pipe smoke at the ceiling. His eyes were squeezed down as he squinted through the smoke.

"If it does, I won't have to look for it anymore."

"Don't look for it anymore." Dramatically, Broz came forward in the swivel chair, his hands flat on the desk. "Stay out of it, or you'll end up looking at the trunk of your car from the inside. You've been warned. Now get the hell out of here." He swiveled the chair around facing the window, putting the high leather back between me and him. What a trouper, I thought.

Phil stood up. I followed him out through the door we'd entered. Broz never moved or said a word. In the anteroom a thin-faced Italian man with a goatee was cleaning his fingernails with the blade of a large pocket knife, his feet up on the desk, a Borsalino hat tipped forward over the bridge of his nose. He paid us no mind as we went through.

• 11 •

I took a cab back from Broz's office to mine. When I got there I sat in my chair in the dark and looked out the window. The snow was steady now and starting to screw up the traffic. Plows were out and their noise added to the normal traffic sounds that drifted up through the closed window. "Sleigh bells ring," I thought, "are ya listening." The falling snow fuzzed out all the lights in the Combat Zone, giving them halos of neon red and streetlight yellow. I was tired. My eye hurt. The knuckles of my left hand were sore and puffy from hitting Sonny in the face. I hadn't eaten for a long time and I was hungry, but I didn't seem to want to eat. I pulled a bottle of bourbon out of the desk drawer and opened it and drank some. It felt hot in my stomach.

Where was I? Somewhere along the line I had touched a nerve and somebody had called Broz. Who? Could be anybody. Broz got around. But it was probably someone today. Broz would have no reason to wait once he knew I was trampling around on his lawn. I couldn't see Broz being tied into the Godwulf Manuscript. It wasn't worth any money. It was impossible to fence. But he'd implied he'd put it back if I dropped out. He knew a lot of people; maybe he could push the right button without being necessarily involved. Maybe he'd been lying. But something had stirred him up. Not only did he want me out of things but he wanted to know what I knew. Maybe it was simply collateral interest. Maybe it was Powell's murder. Maybe he didn't want me digging into that. I liked that better. Terry's description of the two men included one like Sonny. The other one wasn't Phil. But Phil wouldn't do that kind of trench duty, anyway. I was amazed he had done errand duty for me. But why would Broz care one way or the other about a loudmouth kid like Dennis Powell, care enough to send two employees to kill him and frame his girl? Yet somebody's employees did it. It wasn't an amateur job, by Terry's account. Came in, held them up, had her gun, the rubber gloves, the drug they'd brought, the whole thing. It didn't sound like it had been ad libbed. Did they have inside help? How did they get hold of her gun? And what possible interest would Broz have in the university? He had a lot of interests—numbers, women, dope—but higher education didn't seem to be one of them. Of his line, dope would seem the best connection. It seemed the only place where college and Broz overlapped. Dennis Powell was reputed to be a channel for hard stuff: heroin, specifically. That meant, if it were true, that he had mob connections, direct or indirect. Now he was dead, in what looked like some kind of mob killing. And Joe Broz wanted me to keep my nose out of his business.

But what did that have to do with the manuscript? I didn't know. The best connection I had was the dope and the question of the gun. How did they know she'd have a gun there? She'd lived with another girl before she'd lived with Powell. I took another belt of the bourbon. Uncut by bitters or ice and cheap anyway, it grated down into my stomach. Catherine Connelly, Tower had told me. Let's try her. More bourbon. It wasn't really so bad, didn't taste bad at all, made you feel pretty nice in your stomach. Made you feel tough, too, and on top of it—whatever it was. The phone rang.

I picked it up and said, ''Spenser industries, security division. We never sleep.''

There was a pause and then a woman spoke.

"Mr. Spenser?"

"Yeah."

"This is Marion Orchard, Terry's mother."

"Howya doing, sweets," I said, and took another pull on the bourbon.

"Mr. Spenser, she's gone."

"Me, too, sweets."

"No, really, she's gone, and I'm terribly worried."

I put the bottle down and said, "Oh, Christ!"

"Our lawyer called and said the police wish to speak with her again and I went to her room and she wasn't there and she hasn't been home all day. There's two hundred thousand dollars bail money, and . . . I want her back. Can you find her, Mr. Spenser?"

"You got any ideas where I should look?"

"I . . . Mr. Spenser, we have hired you. You sound positively hostile and I resent it."

"Yeah, you probably do," I said. "I been up a long time and have eaten little, and had a fight with a tough guinea and drank too much bourbon and was thinking about going and getting a sub sandwich and going to bed. I'll come out in a little while and we'll talk about it."

"Please, I'm very worried."

"Yeah, I'll be along." I hung up, put the cork in the bottle, put the bottle in the drawer. My head was light and my eyes focused badly and my mouth felt thick. I got my coat on, locked the office, and went down to my car. I parked in a taxi zone and got a submarine sandwich and a large black coffee to go. I ate the sandwich and drank the coffee as I headed out to Newton again. Eating a sub sandwich with one hand is sloppy work and I got some tomato juice and oil on my shirtfront and some coffee stains on my pants leg. I stopped at a Dunkin Donut shop in West Newton Sqaure, bought another black coffee, and sat in my car and drank it.

I felt terrible. The bourbon was wearing off and I felt

dull and sleepy and round-shouldered. I looked at my watch. It was a quarter to ten. The snow continued as I sat and forced the coffee down. I had read somewhere that black coffee won't sober you up, but I never believed it. After bourbon it tasted so awful it had to be doing some good.

The plows hadn't gotten to the Orchards' street; my wheels spun and my car skidded getting up their hill. I had my jacket unbuttoned but the defrosters were going full blast. And, wrestling the car through the snow, I could feel the sweat in the hollow of my back and my shirt collar was wet and limp. Sometimes I wondered if I was getting too old for this work. And sometimes I thought I had gotten too old last year. I jammed the car through a snowdrift into the Orchards' driveway and climbed out. There was no pathway so I waded through the snow across the lawn and up to the front door. The same black maid answered the door. She remembered me, took my hat and coat, and led me to the same library we'd talked in before. A fire was still burning, but no one was in the room. I got a look at myself in the dark window: unshaven, sub sandwich stains on my shirt, collar open. There was a puffy mouse under one eye courtesy of old Sonny. I looked like the leg man for a slumlord.

Marion Orchard came in. She was wearing an ankle-length blue housecoat that zipped up the front, a matching headband, and bare feet. I noticed her toenails were painted silver. She seemed as well groomed and together as before but her face was flushed and I realized she had been drinking. Me, too. Who hadn't? The ride and the coffee had sobered me up and depressed me. My head ached and my stomach felt like I'd been swallowing sand. Without a word Marion Orchard went to the sideboard, put ice in a glass from a silver bucket, added Scotch, and squirted soda in from a silver-laced dispenser. She drank half of it and turned toward me.

"You want some?"

"Yes, ma'am."

"Scotch or bourbon?"

"Bourbon, with bitters if you've got it."

She turned and mixed me bourbon and soda with bitters in a big square-angled glass. I drank some and felt it begin to combat the coffee and the fatigue. I'd need more, though. From the looks of Marion Orchard, she would too, and planned on getting it.

"Where's Mr. Orchard?" I asked.

"At the office. Sitting behind his big masculine desk, trying to feel like a man."

"Does he know Terry's gone?"

"Yes. That's why he went to the office. It makes him feel better about himself. All he can cope with is stocks and bonds. People, and daughters and wives, scare hell out of him." She finished the drink, took mine, which was still half-full, and made two fresh ones.

"Something scares hell out of everybody," I said. "Have you any thoughts on where I should look for Terry?"

"What scares hell out of you?" she asked.

The bourbon was making a lot of headway against the coffee. I felt a lot better than I had when I came in. The line of Marion Orchard's thigh was tight against the blue robe as she sat with her legs tucked up under her on the couch.

"The things people do to one another," I answered. "That scares hell out of me."

She drank some more. "Wrong," she said. "That engages your sympathy. It doesn't scare you. I'm an expert on what scares men. I've lived with a scared man for twenty-two years. I left college in my sophomore year to marry him and I never finished. I was an English major. I wrote poetry. I don't anymore." I waited. She didn't really seem to be talking to me anymore.

"About Terry?" I prodded softly.

"Screw Terry," she said, and finished her drink. "When I was her age I was marrying her father and nobody with wide shoulders came around and got me out of that mess." She was busy making us two more drinks as she talked. Her voice was showing the liquor. She was talking with extra-careful enunciation—the way I was. She handed me the drink and then put her hand on my upper arm and squeezed it.

"How much do you weigh?" she asked.

"One ninety-five."

"You work out, don't you? How much can you lift?"

"I can bench press two-fifty ten times," I said.

"How'd you get the broken nose?" She bent over very carefully and examined my face from about two inches away. Her hair smelled like herbs.

"I fought a ranked heavyweight once."

She stayed bent over, her face two inches away, her fragrant hair tumbling forward, one hand still squeezing my arm, the other holding the drink. I put my left hand behind her head and kissed her. She folded up into my lap and kissed back. It wasn't eager. It was ferocious. She let the glass drop from her hand onto the floor, where I assume it tipped and spilled. Under the blue robe she was wearing nothing at all and she was nowhere near as sinewy as she had looked to me the first time I saw her. Making love in a chair is heavy work. The only other time I'd attempted, I'd gotten a charley horse that damn near ruined the event. With one arm around her back I managed to slip the other one under her knees and pick her up, which is not easy from a sitting position in a soft chair. Her mouth never left mine, nor did the fierceness abate as I carried her to the couch. She bit me and scratched me and at climax she pounded me on the back with her clenched fist as hard as she could. At the time I barely noticed. But when it was over I felt as if I'd been in a fight, and maybe in some sense I had.

She had shed the robe during our encounter and now she walked naked over to the bar to make another drink for each of us. She had a fine body, tanned allover except for the stark whiteness of her buttocks and the thin line her bra strap had made. She returned with a drink in each hand. Gave one to me and then stroked my cheek once, quite gently. She drank half her drink, still standing naked in front of me, and lit a cigarette, took in a long lungful of smoke, let it out, picked up her robe, and slipped into it. There we were all together again, neat, orderly, employee and employer. Here's to you, Mrs. Robinson.

"I think Terry is with a group in Cambridge which calls itself the Ceremony of Moloch. In the past when she would get in trouble or be freaked out on drugs or have a fight with her father she'd run off there and they'd let her stay. One of her friends told me about it."

She'd known that when she'd called me. But she'd gotten me out here to tell me. She really didn't like her husband.

"Where in Cambridge is the Ceremony of Moloch?"

"I don't know. I don't even know if she's there, but it's all I could think of."

"Why did Terry take off?" I didn't use her name. After copulation on the couch, Mrs. Orchard sounded a little silly. On the other hand we were not on a Marion basis.

"A fight with her father." She didn't use my name either.

"About what?"

"What's it ever about? He sees her as an extension of his career. She's supposed to adorn his success by being what he fantasizes a daughter is. She does everything the opposite to punish him for not being what she fantasizes a father is . . . and probably for sleeping with me. Ever read *Mourning Becomes Electra*, Spenser?"

That's how she solved her problem with names; she dropped the Mister. I wondered if I should call her

Orchard. I decided not to. "Yeah, a long time ago. But is there anything you could tell me about Terry, or the Ceremony of Moloch, that might turn out to be useful? It is past midnight and I've gotten a lot of exercise today."

I think she colored very slightly. "You are like a terrier after a rat. Nothing distracts your attention."

"Well," I said, "there are things, occasionally, Marion."

Her color got a little deeper and she smiled, but shook her head.

"I wonder," she said. "I wonder whether you might not have been thinking of a way to run down my dear daughter Terry, even then."

"Then," I said, "I wasn't thinking of anything."

She said, "Maybe."

I was silent. I was so tired it was an effort to move my mouth.

She shook her head again. "No, there's nothing. I can't think of anything else to tell you that will help. But can you look? Can you find her?"

"I'll look," I said. "Did your lawyer tell you what the cops wanted?"

"No. He just said Lieutenant Quirk wanted her to come down tomorrow and talk with him some more."

I stood up. Partly to see if I could. Marion Orchard stood up with me.

"Thank you for coming. I know you'll do you best in finding Terry. I'm sorry to have kept you up so late." She put out her hand and I took it. Christ, breeding. Here she was, upper crust, Boston society, yes'm. Thank you very much, ma'am, for the drink and the toss on the couch, ma'am, it's a pleasure to be of service to you and the master, ma'am. I gave her hand a squeeze. I was goddamned if I was going to shake it.

"I'll dig her up, Marion. When I do I'll bring her home. It'll work out."

She nodded her head silently and her face got congested-looking and red around the eyes and I realized she was going to cry in a minute. I said, "I'll find my way out. Try not to worry. It'll work out."

She nodded again and as I left the library she touched my arm but said nothing. As I closed the door behind me I could hear the first stifled sob burst out. There were more before I got out of earshot. They would probably last most of the night. I went out the front door and into the dead, still white night, got in my car, and went back to town. Every fiber of my being felt awful.

• 12 •

It was about one-thirty when I got back to my apartment. I stripped off my clothes and took a long shower, slowly easing the water temperature down to cool. In the bedroom, putting on clean clothes, I looked at the bed with something approaching lust, but I kept myself away from it. Then I went to the living room in my socks and called a guy I knew who did night duty at the *Globe*. I asked him where I could find the Ceremony of Moloch. He gave me an address in Cambridge. I asked him what he knew about the group.

"Small," he said. "Freaky. Robes and statues and candlelight. That kind of crap. Moloch was some kind of Phoenician god that required human sacrifice. In *Paradise Lost,* Milton lumps him in with Satan and Beelzebub among the fallen angels. That's all I know about them. We did a feature once on the Cambridge-Boston subculture and they got about a paragraph."

I thanked him and hung up and went back into the bedroom for my shoes. I sat down on the bed to put them on and that was where I lost it. As long as I was up I could move, but from sitting to lying was too short a distance. I lay back, just for a minute, and went to sleep.

I woke up, in the same position, nine hours later in broad daylight with the morning gone. I went out to the kitchen, measured out the coffee, put the electric percolator on, went back, stripped down, shaved, showered, put on my shorts, and went out to the kitchen again. The coffee was ready and I drank it with cream and sugar while I sliced peppers and tomatoes for a Spanish omelet.

I felt good. The sleep had taken care of the exhaustion. The snow had stopped and the sunlight, magnified by reflection, was pure white as it splashed about the kitchen. I greased the omelet pan and poured the eggs in. When the inside was right I put in the vegetables and flipped the omelet. I'm very good at flipping omelets. Finding out what was happening with Terry Orchard and the Godwulf Manuscript seemed to be something I wasn't very good at.

I ate the omelet with thick slices of fresh pumpernickel and drank three more cups of coffe while I looked at the morning *Globe*. I felt even better. Okay, Terry Orchard, here I come. You can run, but you can't hide. I considered stopping by to frighten Joe Broz some more but rejected the plan and headed for Cambridge.

The address I had for the Ceremony of Moloch was in North Cambridge in a neighborhood of brown and gray three-decker apartment buildings with open porches across the back of each floor where laundry hung stiff in the cold. I went up the unshoveled path without seeing the print of cloven hoofs. No smell of brimstone greeted me. No darkness visible, no moans of despair. For all I could tell the house was empty and its inhabitants had gone to work or school. Every third person in Cambridge was a student.

In the front hall there were three mailboxes, each with a name plate. The one for the third floor apartment said simply MOLOCH. I went up the stairs without making more noise than I had to and stood outside the apartment door. No sound. I knocked. No answer. I tried the door. Locked. But it was an old door, with the frame warped. About thirty seconds with some thin plastic was all it took to open it.

The door opened onto a narrow hall that ran right and left from it. To the left I could see a kitchen, to the right the half-open door of a bathroom. Diagonally on the other wall an archway opened into a room I couldn't see. The wallpaper in the hall was faded brown fern leaves against a dirty beige background. There were large stains of a darker brown here and there as if someone had splashed water against the walls. The floor was made of narrow hardwood painted dark brown and there was a threadbare red runner the length of the hall. The woodwork was white which had been repainted without being adequately scraped first so that it looked lumpy and pocked. It had not been repainted recently and there were many nicks and gouges in it. I could see part of the tub and part of the water closet in the bathroom. The tub had claw and ball feet and the water closet had a pull chain from the storage tank mounted up by the ceiling. The place was dead still.

I walked through the arch into what must have been the living room. It no longer was. In the bay of the three-window bow along the right-hand wall there was an altar made out of packing crates and two-by-fours which reminded me of the fruit display racks in Faneuil Hall market. It was draped with velveteen hangings in black and crimson and at its highest reach was inverted a dime store crucifix. The crucifix was made of plastic, with the Sacred Heart redly exposed in the center of the flesh-tinted chest. On each side of the crucifix were human skulls. Beside them unmatched candelabras with assorted candles, partially burned. The walls were hung with more of the black velveteen, shabby and thin in the daylight. The floor had been painted black and scattered with cushions. The room smelled strongly of incense and faintly of marijuana and faintly also of unemptied Kitty Litter.

I went back down the corridor through the kitchen with its oilcloth-covered table and its ancient black sink and into a bedroom. There were no beds but five bare mattresses covered the floor. Three of them had sleeping bags rolled neatly at the wall end. In the closet were two pairs of nearly white jeans, a work shirt, something that looked like a shift, and an olive drab undershirt. I couldn't tell if the owners were male or female. The two other bedrooms were much the same. In a pantry closet off the kitchen were maybe a dozen black robes like graduation costumes. On the shelves were a five-pound bag of brown rice, some peanut butter, a loaf of Bond Bread, and a two-pound bag of Granola. In the refrigerator there were a plastic pitcher of grape Kool-Aid, seven cans of Pepsi, and three cucumbers. Maybe they had a bundle in a numbered account in Switzerland but on the surface it didn't look like the Ceremony of Moloch was a high-return venture.

I went back out, closed the door behind me, and went to my car. The noon sun was making the snow melt and heating the inside of my car. I sat in it, two doors up from the house of Moloch, and waited for someone to come there and do something. It was cold and the snow had begun to crust over when someone finally showed up. Eight people, in a battered Volkswagen bus that had been hand-painted green. Three of the eight were girls and one of them was Terry. They all went into what they probably called the temple. I waited some more. I occurred to me that I wasn't exactly sure what to do with Terry now that I'd found her. There wasn't much point in dragging her out by the hair and taking her home locked in the trunk. She'd just take off again and after a while I'd get sick of chasing and fetching.

It was dark now, and cold. A fifteen-year-old Olds-mobile sedan pulled up behind the Volkswagen bus and unloaded five more people. They went into the three-decker. I sat some more. The thing to do was to call Marion Orchard, tell her I'd located her daughter, have her notify the cops, and let them bring her in. I had no legal authority to go in and get her. No question. That was what I should do. I looked at my watch, 7:15.

I slipped out of my coat, got out of the car, and went to the house of the Ceremony of Moloch. This time I was very quiet going up the stairs. At the door I stood silent and listened. I could hear music that sounded as if it were being played on one string of an Armenian banjo. The smell of incense and pot was very rich. At irregular intervals there were chimes like the ones rung during a Roman Catholic Mass. The thing to do was to call Terry's mother and have the cops come pick her up. I took out my plastic shim and opened the door. Inside the hallway the heat was tangible and stifling. There was no light.

From the living-room altar area came the twanging sound of the music, now quite loud, and the lesser sound of a man chanting. A flickering light fell into the hallway from the living room. Despite the heat I felt cold and my throat was tight. The chimes sounded again. And I heard a kind of muffled whimper, like someone sobbing into a pillow. I looked carefully around the corner. Suspended by clothesline from the ceiling, in front of the altar I had seen earlier was a full-sized cross, made of two-by-sixes. To it, in a parody of the Crucifixion, Terry Orchard was tied with more length of clothesline. She was naked and her body had been marked with astrological and cabalistic signs in what looked to be, in the candlelight, several different colors of magic marker. She was gagged with a wide piece of gray tape.

Before her stood a tall wiry man, naked too, wearing a black hood, his body covered with the same kind of magic marker design work. In a semicircle on the floor, in black robes, sat the rest of the people. The music was coming from a tape recorder behind the altar. In his hand the guy with the hood had a carved piece of black wood, about a foot and a half long, that looked like a nightstick. He was chanting in a monotonous singsong in a language I didn't understand and didn't recognize. And as he chanted he swayed in front of Terry in an approximation of the beat from the tape recorder. The seated audience rocked back and forth in the same tempo. Then he made a gesture with the nightstick and I realized its function was phallic.

I took out my gun and put a bullet into the tape recorder. The explosion of the shot and the cessation of the music were simultaneous, and the silence that followed was paralyzing. I stepped into the room with my gun leveled at all of them, but especially the fruitcake with the hood. With my left hand I took a jackknife out of my pants pocket, and worked the blade open with one hand by holding it in my teeth. No one made a sound. I sidestepped around behind the cross and cut Terry loose without taking my eyes from the audience. When the ropes parted she fell. I folded the knife shut against my leg and put it away. I reached down without looking and got her up with one hand under her arm. The guy with the hood and the funny nightstick never took his eyes off me, and the steady gaze through the Halloween pumpkin triangles cut in the hood made me very edgy. So did the fact that there was one of me and twelve of them.

My hand still hanging on to Terry's arm, I backed up out of the room, through the narrow hall, and out the still-open door. The cold air of the stairwell rushed up like the wind from an angel's wing in the doorway of Hell.

"I'm going to close this door," I said, and my voice sounded like someone else's. "If it opens I'll shoot at it."

No one said a word. No one moved. I let go of Terry's arm, closed the door, took hold of her arm again, and headed down the stairs. No one came after us. Out the front door and across to my car. We ran. In my mind I could see us from their third floor vantage, outlined sharp against the white snow in the streetlight. No one shot at us. I pushed Terry into the car first, came in behind her, and got it out of there. It was a full block before I looked at Terry. She huddled, still stark naked, still with the tape on her mouth, in the far corner of the seat. She must have been freezing. I reached into the back seat, took my coat from where I'd left it, and gave it to her. She pulled it around her.

"Maybe you ought to take the gag off," I said.

She peeled it off carefully, and spit out what looked like a wadded paper towel which had been stuffed in her mouth. She didn't say anything. I didn't say anything. The heater had warmed up and was starting to warm the car. I turned on the radio. We went down along the Charles on Memorial Drive and across the Mass Ave bridge. Boston always looks great from there. Especially at night with the lights and the skyline against the starry sky and the sweep of the river in a graceful curve down toward the harbor. It probably didn't look too spiffy at the moment to Terry.

I turned off onto Marlborough Street and pulled up in front of my apartment. Terry waited in the car while I went around and opened the door. She was well brought up. She had to walk barefoot across the frozen pavement but showed no sign that she felt it. We went up in the elevator.

Inside my apartment she looked about curiously. As if we'd recently met at a cocktail party and I'd invited her home to see my carvings. I felt the urge to giggle hysterically, but stifled it. I went to the kitchen, got out some ice, and poured two big shots of bourbon over the ice. I gave her one. Then I went to the bathroom and started to run hot water in the tub. She stayed right behind me—like a dog I used to have when it was supper time, or he thought I might be about to go somewhere.

"Get in," I said. "Take a long, slow hot bath. Drink another drink. I'll make us some supper, and we'll eat it together. No candlelight, though. A lot of bright overheads."

I took her nearly empty glass, added more ice, and filled it again. I gave it to her, pushed her gently into the bathroom, and closed the door.

"There's some kind of bubble bath or whatever in the

102

medicine cabinet," I said through the door. I waited till I heard her splash into the tub. Then I went to the kitchen. I put on a pot of rice to cook and got four boneless chicken breasts out of the meat keeper. I cooked them with wine and butter and cream and mushrooms. While they cooked I tossed a salad and made a dressing with lime juice and mint, olive oil, honey, and wine vinegar. There were two bottles of Rhine wine in the refrigerator for which I'd originally had other plans, but I could buy some more tomorrow.

By the time I'd gotten the table set in the living room, she was through, and came out of the bathroom wearing a towel with her hair tucked up and some color in her face. I handed her my bathrobe and she slipped into it, modestly closing it before she let the towel slip to the floor. It occurred to me that half the time we'd spent together she'd been without clothes.

I gave her a third drink and freshened up my own. She sat on a stool in the kitchen and sipped it while I put some baking powder biscuits in the oven.

She had not spoken since I'd found her. Now she said, "Do you have any cigarettes?"

I found some thin filter tips in a fancy feminine package that a friend had left in one of the kitchen drawers. I held a match for her as she lit one and inhaled deeply. She let the smoke slip slowly out of her nose as she sipped her drink, holding the glass in both hands. The smoke spread out on the surface of the bourbon and eddied gently back up around her face. I felt my stomach tighten; I had known someone a long time ago who used to do just that, in just that way.

I got out the corkscrew and opened one of the bottles of wine. I poured some into each glass, and then took the biscuits out and served the supper. She sat opposite me at the small table and ate. Her manners were terrific. One hand in the lap, small bites, delicate sips of wine. But she ate everything. So did I. Still no talk. I had the radio on in the kitchen. When I offered her more, she nodded yes. When I got up to get the second bottle of wine I plugged in the coffee. Its steady perk made a pleasant counterpoint to the radio. When we'd finished eating, I poured the coffee and brought out some applejack and two pony glasses. I put them on the cobbler's bench coffee table in front of the sofa. She sat at one end and I sat at the other, and we drank out coffee and sipped our brandy and she smoked another cigarerette, holding her hand primly over the gap in the front of the bathrobe as she leaned over to accept my light. I got out a cigar and we listened some more to the radio. She leaned back against the arm of the couch and closed her eyes.

I stood up and said, "You can sleep in my bed. I'll sleep out here." I walked to the bedroom door and opened it. She went in.

I said, "I'm sorry I don't have any pajamas. You could sleep in one of my dress shirts, I guess."

"No, thank you," she said. "I don't wear anything to bed anyway."

"Okay," I said. "Good night. We'll talk in the morning."

She went in and shut the door, then opened it a crack. I heard her get into the bed. I picked up the dishes and put them in the dishwasher. Then I went in and took a shower and shaved. I felt odd, like my father probably had when we were small and all home and in bed and he was the only one up in the house. I got a blanket out of the closet, shut out the lights, and lay on my back on the couch smoking the rest of my cigar, blowing the smoke across the glowing tip.

I heard the light click on in the bedroom. She called, "Spenser?"

"Yeah?"

"Would you come in here, please?"

I got up, put on a pair of pants, and went in, still smoking the cigar. She was lying on her back in bed with covers pulled up under her chin.

"Sit on the bed," she said.

I did.

"Did you ever work on a farm?" she asked me.

"Nope."

"My grandfather, my mother's father, had a farm in Illinois. He used to milk fifty cows a day and he had forearms like yours. He wasn't as big as you but he had muscles in his forearms like you do."

I nodded.

"You're not fat at all, are you?" she said. I shook my head.

"With your clothes on you look as if you might be a little fat, but with your shirt off you're not. It's all muscle, isn't it?"

I nodded.

"You look like . . . like a boxer, or like somebody in a Tarzan movie."

"Cheetah," I said.

"Do you know," she said, "do you know that I've only met you four times in my life and you are the only person in the entire world I can trust?" As she got to the end of the sentence her eyes filled. I patted her leg and said, "Shhh." But she went on, her voice not quite steady but apparently under control.

"Dennis is dead. My mother and father use me to get even with each other. I thought I could join the Moloch people. They'd dropped out, they weren't hung up on all the crap my father is. I thought they just took you as you were. They don't." Her voice got shakier. "They initiate you."

I patted her thigh again. I had nothing to say. The stub of the cigar was too short. I put it in an ashtray on the night table.

"Do you know what the initiation is?"

"I figured out the first part," I said.

She sat up in bed and let the covers fall away.

"You are the only one in the world, in the whole goddamned sonova bitch world . . ." The tears started to come. I leaned toward her and put my arm around her and she caught hold of me and squeezed.

"Love me," she said in a choked voice. "Make love to me, make me feel, make love to me, make me feel." A fleeting part of my mind thought, "Jesus, first the mother, then the daughter," but the enduring majority of my mind said, "Yes, Yes, Yes," as I bore her back onto the bed and turned the covers back from her.

13

In the morning I drove Terry home. Riding out to Newton we mentioned neither the Ceremony of Moloch nor the previous night. We ran through the events of the murder again, nothing new. I described Sonny for her in detail. Yes, that sounded like one of the men. They had brought the drug with them that she'd swallowed. They had brought her gun with them. Yes, she had shared that apartment with Cathy Connelly before Dennis had moved in. They had parted friends and still were, as far as Terry knew. Cathy lived on the Fenway, she said. On the museum side near the end closest to the river. She didn't know the number. I stopped in front of her house and let her out. I didn't go in. Having slept with mother and daughter within the same twenty-four hours, I felt fussy about sitting around with both of them in the library and making small talk. She leaned back in through the open door of my car.

"Call me," she said.

"I will," I said.

She closed the door and I pulled away, watching her in the rear view mirror. She went in very slowly, turning once to wave at me. I tooted the horn in reply.

Back to Boston again. I seemed to be making this drive a lot. Turning off Storrow at the Charlesgate exit, I went up the ramp over Commonwealth Ave and looked down at the weeping willows underneath the arch—bare now, with slender branches crusted in snow and bending deep beneath winter weight. There was a Frost poem, but it was about birches, and then I was off the ramp and looking for a parking space. This was not a business for poets anyway.

I parked near the Westland Avenue entrance to the Fenway and walked across the street to a drugstore. There was no listing in the phone book for a Catherine Connelly on the Fenway. So I started at the north end and began looking at the mailboxes in apartment lobbies, working my way south toward the museum. In the third building I found it. Second floor. I rang. Nothing happened. I rang again and leaned on it. No soap. I rang some other buzzers at random. No one opened the door. A cagey lot. I rang all the buttons. No response. Then a mean, paunchy man in green twill shirt and pants came to the front door. He opened it about a foot and said, "Whaddya want?"

"You the super?" I said.

"Who do you think I am?" He was smoking a cigarette that looked as if he'd found it, and it waggled wetly in the corner of his mouth as he spoke.

"I thought you were one of Santa's helpers coming around to see if everything was set for Christmas."

"Huh?" he said.

"I'm looking for a young woman named Catherine Connelly. She doesn't answer her bell," I said.

"Then she ain't home."

"Mind if I check?"

"You better stop ringing them other buzzers too," he said, and shut the door. I resisted the temptation to ring all the buzzers again and run. "Childish," I thought. "Adolescent." I went back to my car, got in, and drove to the university. Maybe I'd be able to locate her there. I parked in a spot that was reserved for Dean Mersfelder and headed for the library basement.

Iris Milford was there in her NEWS office, behind her metal desk. There were several other members of the staff, obviously younger, doing journalistic things at their metal desks.

She recognized me when I came in.

"Nice eye you got," she said.

I'd forgotten the punch Sonny had landed. It looked worse than it felt, though it was still sore to touch.

"I bruise easily," I said.

"I'll bet," she said.

"Want to have lunch with me?" I asked.

"Absolutely," she said. She closed the folder she was looking at, picked up her purse, and came around the desk.

"Too bad about how you can't make up your mind," I said.

We walked out through the corridor. It was class-change time and the halls were crowded and hot and loud. A miasma of profanity and smoke and sweatiness under heavy winter coats. Ah, where are the white bucks of yesteryear? We wormed our way up to the first floor and finally out past the security apparatus that set off an alarm if someone smuggled out a book, past the scrutiny of a hard-faced librarian alert beside it, into the milling snow-crusted quadrangle. I got a cab and we rode to a restaurant I liked on top of an insurance building, where the city looked clean and patrician below, and the endless rows of red-brick town houses that had crumbled into slums looked geometric and orderly and a little European, stretching off to the south.

We had a drink and ordered lunch. Iris looked out at the orderly little brick houses.

"Get far enough away and it looks kinda pretty, don't it?" she said. "You only get order from a distance. Close up is always messy."

"Yeah," I said, "but your own life is always close up. You only see other people's lives at long range."

"You better believe it," she said. "I'll take another pop."

I ordered us two more drinks.

"Okay, Spenser, what is it? You not the type to feed drinks to a poor colored lady and take advantage of her body. Even one as irresistible as mine. What you want?"

I liked her. She'd been there and seen it done. A tough, wised-up honest broad.

"Well, if you're not going to come across, I'll take second best. Tell me about Cathy Connelly."

"What you want to know?"

"I don't know, everything, anything. All I know is she was once Terry Orchard's roommate, that she moved out when the Powell kid moved in, that she now lives on the Fenway, and that she wasn't home when I called on her this morning."

"That's about as much as I know. She was in my Chaucer class, and I copied her notes a couple times. I don't know her much better than that."

"She belong to SCACE?"

"Not that I know. She seemed kind of a loner. Didn't belong to anything I know of. You never see her around campus, but that don't mean much because the goddamn campus is so big and crowded that you might not see a woolly rhinoceros around campus."

"Boy friends?" I asked.

"None that I know. But I'm telling you, I don't hardly know her. What I'm saying could be wrong as hell."

"Where can I get a picture of her?"

"Student Personnel Office, I would guess. That's where we get ones we use in the paper for fast-breaking news stories like who was elected captain of the girl's field hockey team. Campus security can probably get them for you."

"I don't think so, Iris. Last dealings I had with campus security was when they ejected me from the premises. I think they don't like me."

She widened her eyes. "I thought they hired you."

"They did, but I think they are in the process of making

an agonizing reappraisal of that decision.''

''You having a good week, Spenser. Someone plunks you in the eye, you get thrown off the campus, you gonna get fired, you can't find Cathy Connelly. I hope you don't depress easy.''

''Like you were saying, it's always messy close up.''

''What you want Connelly for, anyway?''

''She was Terry Orchard's roommate. She might know how Terry's gun got from her bedside table into a hood's pocket.''

''Jesus, she don't look the type.''

''There isn't any type, my love.''

She nodded, ''Ain't that the truth.''

''Want dessert?'' I said.

She nodded. ''Do I look like someone who turns down dessert?''

I asked for a dessert menu.

Iris said, ''I can get the picture for you. I'll go over to student personnel and tell them we need it for a feature we're doing. We do it all the time.''

''Would you like two desserts?'' I said.

After I paid the bill with some of Roland Orchard's retainer and drove her back to the university, she did what she said. I sat in the car with the heater on and she strolled into the student center and returned twenty minutes later with a two-by-two ID photo of Cathy Connelly. I thanked her.

She said, ''Two drinks and a lobster salad will get you almost anything, baby,'' and went to class.

I drove over to Mass Ave and had a technician I know at a photo lab blow the picture up to eight by ten. Service while I waited cost me twenty-five dollars more of Roland Orchard's retainer, and I still hadn't got the tear fixed in my car top.

I took the picture back to my office and sat behind my desk looking at it. She looked like a pallid little girl. Small features, light hair, prominent teeth, serious eyes. While I was looking at her picture my door opened and in came Lieutenant Quirk. Hatless, wearing a glen plaid overcoat, shoes glossy, pocked face clean-shaven, ruddy from the cold, and glowing with health. He closed the door behind him and stood looking at me with his hands in his overcoat pockets. He did not radiate cheer.

"Come in, Lieutenant," I said. "No need to knock, my door is always open to a public servant. You've come no doubt to ask my assistance in solving a particularly knotty puzzle . . ."

"Knock it off, Spenser. If I want to listen to bullshit, I'll go over to a City Council meeting."

"Okay, have a seat. Want a drink?"

Quirk ignored the chair I'd nodded at and stood in front of my desk.

"Yeah, I'll have a drink."

I poured two shots of bourbon into two paper cups. Quirk drank his off without expression and put the empty cup down. I sipped at mine a little and thought fondly of the stuff that Roland Orchard served.

"Terry Orchard is it, Spenser," he said.

"The hell she is."

"She's it. Captain Yates is taking personal charge of the case, and she's the one."

"Yates. That means you're off it?"

"That's right."

"What else does it mean?"

"It doesn't mean anything else."

I poured two more shots of bourbon. Quirk's hard face looked like he was concealing a toothache.

"Like hell it doesn't mean anything else, Quirk. You didn't make a special trip down here just to keep me informed on personnel shifts in the BPD. You don't like her for it and you know it. Why is Yates on it?"

"He didn't say."

I sipped some more of my bourbon. Quirk walked over and looked out my window.

"What a really swell view you've got, Spenser."

I didn't say anything. Quirk came back to my desk, picked up the bottle, and poured himself another drink.

"Okay," he said. "I don't like the kid for the murder."

I said, "Me either."

"I got nothing. Everything I've got says she's guilty. Nice simple murder, nice simple solution. Why screw around with it?"

"That's right," I said. "Why screw around with it?"

"I've been on the force twenty-two years. You meet a lot of liars in twenty-two years. I don't think she was lying."

I said, "Me either."

Quirk was walking around the room as he talked, looking at it like he looked at everything, seeing it all, and if he ever had to he'd remember it all.

"You went to see Joe Broz yesterday."

I nodded.

"Why?"

"So he could tell me to butt out of the Godwulf Manuscript-Terry Orchard affair."

"What did you say?"

"I said we'll see."

"Did you know the manuscript is back?"

I raised one eyebrow, something I'd perfected after years of practice and a score of old Brian Donlevy movies. Quirk appeared not to notice.

"Broz suggested that was possible," I said.

Quirk nodded. "Any idea why Broz wanted you to butt out?"

"No," I said. "Any idea why Yates wanted you to butt out?"

"No, but there's a lot of pressure from somewhere up the line."

"And Yates is responding."

Quirk's face seemed to shut down. "I don't know about what Yates is doing. I know he's in charge of the case and I'm not. He's the captain. He has the right to assign personnel."

"Yeah, sure. I know Yates a little. One of the things he does best is respond to pressure from somewhere up the line."

Quirk didn't say anything.

"Look, Lieutenant," I said, "does it seem odd to you that there are two guys looking into the Terry Orchard thing and both of us are told to butt out within the same day? Does that seem like any kind of coincidence to you?"

"Spenser, I am a cop. I have been a cop for twenty-two years and I will keep on being one unil they lock me out of the station house. One of the things that a cop has to have is discipline. He gets orders, he has to obey them or the whole thing goes to hell. I don't have to like what's happening, but I do it. And I don't run around crying about it."

"Words to live by," I said. "It was the widely acclaimed Adolf Eichmann who popularized that 'I obey orders' routine, wasn't it?"

"That's a cheap shot, Spenser. You know goddamn well the cops are right more than they're wrong. We're not wiping out six million people. We're trying to keep the germs from taking over the world. To do that you got to have order and if someone gets burned now and then so someone gets burned. If every cop started deciding which order to obey and which one not, then the germs would win. If the germs win, all the goddamn bleeding hearts will get their ass shot."

"Yeah, sure, the big picture. So some goddamn teen-age kid gets fed to the fishes for something she didn't do. So you know she didn't do it and Joe Broz puts the squeeze on some politician who puts the squeeze on Captain Yates who takes you off the case. But you don't cry. It's good for society. Balls. Why don't you take what you got to the States?''

"Because I haven't got enough. The State cops would laugh and giggle if I came in with what I've got. And because, goddamn it, Spenser, because I can't. I'm a cop. It's what I do. I can't.''

"I know,'' I said. "But I can. And I'm going to. I'm going to have Broz and Yates, and you too, if I have to, and whoever else has got his thumb in whatever pie this is.''

"Maybe you will,'' Quirk said. "I hear you were a pretty good cop before you got fired. What'd you get fired for?''

"Insubordination. It's one of my best things.''

"And maybe Broz will have you shot in the back of the head.''

I let that pass. We were silent.

"How much do I have to get for you before you go to the States?''

"I'm not asking you to get a damn thing for me,'' Quirk said.

"Yeah, I know. If I got you proof. Not suspicion, proof. Then what happens?''

"Then the pressure will go away. Yates is impressed with proof.''

"I'll bet,'' I said.

More silence. Quirk didn't seem to want to leave, but he didn't have anything to say. Or at least he wasn't saying it.

"What do you know about Cathy Connelly, Lieutenant?''

"We checked her out routinely. No record, no evidence of drugs. Roomed with Orchard before her boy friend moved in. Now lives somewhere over on the Fenway.''

"Anybody interview her?''

"Couple of precinct boys in a radio car stopped by. She wasn't home. We saw no reason to press it. Do you?"

"Those two hoods had Terry Orchard's gun with them when they came to the apartment. How'd they get it?"

"If it's true."

"Of course, if it's true. I think it's true. Cathy Connelly seems like the best person to ask about how they got the gun. Terry doesn't know, Powell is dead. Who's left?"

"Why don't you go ask her then?" Quirk said. "Thanks for the drink."

He walked out leaving the door open behind him and I listened to his footsteps going down the hall.

14

I went over to the university to call on Carl Tower. I hoped the campus cops weren't under orders to shoot on sight. Whether they were, the secretary with the ripe thighs was not. She was friendly. She had on a pants suit today, black, with a large red valentine heart over the left breast. Red platform heels, red enamel pendant earrings. Bright red lipstick. She obviously remembered me. I was probably haunting her dreams.

She said, "May I help you?"

"Don't pull that sweet talk on me," I said.

"I beg your pardon."

"I know what you're thinking, and I'm sorry, but I'm on duty."

"Of all the outer offices in all the towns in all the world," she said, "you had to walk into mine." There was no change in her expression.

I started to say something about, "If you want anything, just whistle," but at that moment Carl Tower appeared at his office door and saw me. I was obviously not haunting his dreams.

"Spenser," he said, "get the hell in my office."

I took off my wrist watch and gave it to the secretary. "If I don't come out alive," I said, "I want you to have this."

She giggled. I went into Tower's office.

Tower picked up a tabloid-sized newspaper from his desk and tossed it across at me. It was the university newspaper. Across the top was a headline, "AD-MINISTRATION AGENT SPIES ON STUDENT," and in a smaller drop head, "PRIVATE EYE HIRED BY ADMINISTRATION QUESTIONS ENGLISH PROFESSOR." I didn't bother to read the story, though I noticed they spelled my name wrong in the lead paragraph.

"It's with an *s*, not a *c*," I said. "Like the English poet. S-p-e-n-s-e-r."

Tower was biting down so hard on his back teeth that the muscles of his jaw bulged at the hinge.

"We won't ask for a return on the retainer, Spenser," he said. "But if you are on this campus again, ever, we'll arrest you for trespassing and use every influence we have to have your license lifted."

"I hear you got the manuscript back," I said.

"That's right. No thanks to you. Now beat it."

"Who returned it?"

"It just showed up yesterday in a cardboard box, on the library steps."

"Ever wonder why it came back?"

Tower stood up. "You're through, Spenser. As of this minute. You are no longer in the employ of this university. You have no business here. You're trespassing. Either you leave or I call some people to take you out of here."

"How many you going to call?"

Tower's face got quite red. He said, "You sonova bitch," and put his hand on the phone.

I said, "Never mind. If I whipped your entire force it would embarrass both of us."

On the way out I stopped by the secretary's desk. She handed me back my watch.

"I'm glad you made it," she said.

On the inside of the watch strap in red ink she had written "Brenda Loring, 437-3676."

I looked up at her. "I am, too," I said, and strapped the watch back on.

She went back to typing and I went back to leaving the university in disgrace. Administration agent, I thought as I went furtively down the corridor. Zowie!

15

Back to the Fenway to Cathy Connelly's apartment. I rang
the bell, no answer. I didn't feel like swapping com-
pliments with Charlie Charm the super, so I strolled
around the building looking for an alternate solution.
Behind the apartment was an asphalt coutyard with lines
for parking spaces and a line of trash barrels, dented and
bent, against the wall, behind low trapezoidal concrete
barriers to keep the cars from denting and bending them
more. Despite the ill-fitting covers on them, some of the
trash had spilled out and littered the ground along the
foundation. The cellar entrance door was open but the
screen door was closed and fastened with a hook and eye
arrangement. It was plastic screening. I took out my
jackknife and cut through the screen at the hook. I put my
hand through and unhooked it. Tight security, I thought.
Straight ahead and two steps down stretched the cellar. To
my left rose the stairs. I went up them. Cathy Connelly
was apartment 13. I guessed second floor, given the size
of the building. I was wrong. It was third floor. Close
observation is my business.

Down the corridor ran a frayed, faded rose runner. The
doors were dark-veneer wood with the numbers in shiny
silver decals asymmetrically pasted on. The knob on each
door was fluted glass. The corridor was weakly lit by a
bare bulb in a wall sconce at the end. In front of number 13
a faint apron of light spread out under the door. I looked at
my watch, 4:30. It wouldn't be daylight. I knocked. No
answer. I knocked again. Same result. I put my ear against

the door panel. The television was on, or the radio. I heard no other sound. That didn't prove anything. Lots of people left the TV running when they went out. Some to discourage burglars. Some because they forgot to turn them off. Some so it wouldn't seem so empty when they came home. I tried the knob. No soap. The door was locked. That was a problem about as serious as the screen door in the cellar. I kicked it open—which would probably irritate the super, since when I did, the jamb splintered. I stepped in and felt the muscles begin to tighten behind my shoulders. The apartment was hot and stuffy and there was a smell I'd smelled before.

The real estate broker had probably described it as a studio apartment—which meant one room with kitchenette and bath. The bath was to my left, door slightly ajar. The kitchenette was directly before me, separated from the rest of the room by a plastic curtain. To my right were a day bed, the covers folded back as if someone were about to get in, an armchair with a faded pink and beige shawl draped over it as a slipcover, a bureau, a steamer trunk apparently used as a coffee table, and a wooden kitchen table, painted blue, which seemed to double as a desk. On it the television maundered in black and white. In front of the kitchen table was a straight chair. A woman's white blouse and faded denim skirt were folded over the back of it, underwear and socks tangled on the seat. A saddle shoe lay on its side beneath the chair and another stood flat-footed under the table. There was no one in the room. There was no one behind the plastic curtain. I turned into the bathroom and found her.

She was in the tub, face down, her head under water, her body beginning to bloat. The smell was stronger in here. I forced myself to look. There was a clotted tangle of blood in the hair back of one ear. I touched the water, it was room temperature. Her body was the same. I wanted to turn her over, but I couldn't make myself do it. On the

121

floor by the tub, looking as if she'd just stepped out of them, were a pair of flowered baby doll pajamas. She'd been there awhile. Couple of days anyway. While I'd been ringing her bell and asking the super if he'd seen her, she'd been right here, floating motionless in the tepid water. How do you do, Miss Connelly, my name is Spenser, very sorry I didn't get to meet you sooner. Hell of a way to meet now. I looked at her for two, maybe three minutes, feeling the nausea bubble inside me. Nothing happened, so I began to look at the bathroom. It was crummy. Plastic tiles, worn linoleum buckling up from the floor. The sink was dirty and the faucet dripped steadily. There was no shower. Big patches of paint had peeled off the ceiling. I thought of a line from a poem: "Even the dreadful martyrdom must run its course/Anyhow in a corner, some untidy spot." I forget who wrote it.

There were no telltale cigar butts, no torn halves of claim checks, no traces of lint from an imported cashmere cloth sold only by J. Press. No footprints, no thumb prints, no clues. Just a drowned kid swelling with death in a shabby bathroom in a crummy appartment in a lousy building run by a grumpy janitor. And me.

I went back out into the living room. No phone. God is my copilot. I went out to the hall and down the stairs to the cellar. The super had an office partitioned off with chicken wire from the rest of the cellar. In it were a rolltop desk, an antique television set, and a swivel chair, in which sat the super. The smell of bad wine oozed out of the place. He looked at me with no sign of recognition or welcome.

I said, "I want to use your phone."

He said, "There's a pay phone at the drugstore across the street. I ain't running no charity here."

I said, "There is a dead person in room thirteen and I am going to call the police and tell them. If you say anything to me but *yes, sir* I will hit you at least six times in the face."

He said, "Yes, sir." Pushing an old wino around always enlivens your spirits. I picked up the phone and called Quirk. Then I went back upstairs and waited for him to arrive with his troops. It wasn't as long a wait as it seemed. When they arrived Captain Yates was along.

He and Quirk went in to look at the remains. I sat on the day bed and didn't look at anything. Sergeant Belson sat on the edge of the table smoking a short cigar butt that looked like he'd stepped on it.

"Do you buy those things secondhand?" I asked.

Belson took the cigar butt out of his mouth and looked at it. "If I smoked the big fifty cent jobs in the cedar wrappers you'd figure I was on the take."

"Not the way you dress," I said.

"You ever think of another line of work, Spenser? So far all you've detected is two stiffs. Maybe a crossing guard, say, or . . ."

Quirk and Yates came out of the bathroom with a man from the coroner's. The lines in Quirk's face looked very deep and the medic was finishing a shrug. Yates came over to me. He was a tall man with narrow shoulders and a hard-looking pot belly. He wore glasses with translucent plastic rims like they used to hand out in the army. His mouth was wide and loose.

He looked at me very hard and said, "Someone's going to have to pay for that door."

Belson gave him a startled look; Quirk was expressionless. I couldn't think of anything to say, so I didn't say anything. It was a technique I ought to work on.

Yates said, "What's your story, Jack? What the hell are you doing here?"

"Spenser," I said, "with an *s* like the English poet. I was selling Girl Scout cookies door to door and they told us to be persistent . . ."

"Don't get smart with me, Jack; we got you for breaking and entering. If the lieutenant here hadn't said he knew you I'd a run you in already. The janitor says you threatened him, too."

I looked at Belson. He was concentrating mightily on getting his cigar butt relit, turning it carefully over the flame of a kitchen match to make sure it fired evenly. He didn't look at me.

"What's the coroner's man say about the kid?" I asked Quirk.

Yates answered, "Accidental death. She slipped getting in the tub, hit her head, and drowned." Belson made a noise that sounded like a cough. Yates spun toward him. "You got something to say, Sergeant?"

Belson looked up. "Not me, Captain, no, sir, just inhaled some smoke wrong. Fell right on her head, all right, yes, sir."

Yates stared at Belson for about fifteen seconds. Belson puffed on his cigar. His face showed nothing. Quirk was looking carefully at the light fixture in the ceiling.

"Captain," I said, "does it bother you that her bed is turned back, her clothes are on the chair, and her pajamas are on the bathroom floor? Does it seem funny to you that someone would take off her clothes, put on her pajamas, walk across the room, take off her pajamas, and get in the bathtub?"

"She brought them in to put on when she got through," Yates said very quickly. His mouth moved erratically as he talked. It was like watching a movie with the soundtrack out of sync. Peculiar.

"And dropped them carefully in a pile on the floor where the tub would splash them and she'd drip on them when she got out because she loved putting on wet pajamas," I said.

"Accidental death by drowning. Open and shut." Yates said it hard and loud with a lot of lip motion. Fascinating to watch. "Quirk, let's go. Belson, get this guy's statement. And you, Jack—" he gave me the hard

124

look again—''be where I can reach you. And when I call, you better come running.''

''How about I come over and sleep on your back step,'' I said, but Yates was already on his way out.

Quirk looked at Belson. Belson said, ''Right on her head she fell, Marty.''

Quirk said, ''Yeah,'' and went out after Yates.

Belson whistled ''The Battle Hymn of the Republic'' between his teeth as he got out his notebook and looked at me. ''Shoot,'' he said.

''For crissake, Frank, this is really raw.''

''Captain don't want an editorial,'' Belson said, ''just what happened.''

''Even if you aren't bothered by the pajamas and all, isn't it worth more than routine when the ex-roommate of a murder suspect dies violently?''

Belson said, ''I spent six years rattling doorknobs under the MTA tracks in Charlestown. Now I ride in a car and wear a tie. Captain just wants what happened.''

I told him.

• 16 •

I sat in my car on the dark Fenway. The super had, grumb-
ling, installed a padlock on the splintered door to the
Connelly apartment while a prowl car cop watched.
Belson had departed with my statement and everything
was neat and orderly again. The corpse gone. The mob,
the cops, the university had all told me to mind my own
business. Not a bad trio; I was waiting for a threat from
organized religion. In a few weeks Terry Orchard would
be gone, to the women's reformatory in Framingham,
twenty years probably, a crime of passion by a young
woman. She'd be out when she was forty, ready to start
anew. You meet such interesting people in jail.

I got a flashlight and some tape out of the glove com-
partment and a pinch bar out of my trunk and went back
over to the apartment house. The super hadn't fixed the
screen on the back door, but he had shut and locked the
inside door. I went to a cellar window. It was locked. On
my hands and knees I looked through the frost patterns of
grime. Inside was darkness. I flashed the light through.
Inside was what looked like a coal bin, no longer used for
coal. There were barrels, and boxes, and a couple of
bicycles. I taped a tic-tac-toe pattern on one of the
windowpanes and tapped the glass out with the pinch bar.
The tape kept the noise down. When the opening was big
enough I reached my hand through and unlatched the
window. It was not a very big window but I managed to
slide through it, and drop to the cellar floor. I scraped both
shins in the process.

The cellar was a maze of plastic trash bags, old wooden barrels, steamer trunks, cardboard boxes, clumsily tied piles of newspaper. A rat scuttled out of the beam from my flashlight as I worked my way through the junk. At the far end a door, slightly ajar, opened onto the furnace room and to the left were the stairway and the super's cage. I could hear canned laughter from the television. I went very quietly along the wall toward the stairs. I was in luck; when I peered around the corner of the super's office he was in his swivel chair asleep in the rich fumes of port wine and furnace heat, the TV blaring before him. I went up the same stairs to the third floor. No hesitation on the second floor—I learn quickly. The padlock on Cathy Connelly's door was cheap and badly installed. I got the pinch bar under the hasp and pulled it loose with very little noise. Once inside I put a chair against the door to keep it closed, and turned on the lights. The place hadn't changed much in the past two hours. The bloated corpse was gone, but otherwise there was nothing different. It wasn't a very big apartment. I could search it in a couple of hours probably. I didn't know what I was looking for, of course, which would slow me down, because I couldn't eliminate things on an "is-it-bigger-than-a-bread-box" basis.

I started in the bathroom, because it was on the left. If you are going to get something searched you have to do it orderly. Start at a point and go section by section through the place, not where things are most likely, or least likely, or anything else, just section by section until you've looked at everything. The bathroom didn't take long. There were in the medicine cabinet some toothpaste, some aspirin, some nose drops prescribed by a doctor in New Rochelle, New York, a bottle of Cope, some lipstick, some liquid make-up, a safety razor, an eyebrow pencil. I emptied out the make-up bottle, there was nothing in it but make-up. The aspirin tasted like aspirin, the Cope appeared to be Cope, the nose drops smelled like nose drops. There was nothing in the lipstick tube but lipstick. There was nothing in the toilet tank, nothing taped underneath the sink, no sign that anything had been slipped under the buckling linoleum. I stood on the toilet seat and unscrewed the ceiling fixture with a jackknife blade—nothing inside but dusty wiring that looked like it wouldn't pass the city's electrical code. I screwed the fixture back in place.

I went over the kitchen next. I emptied the flour, sugar, dry cereal, salt, and pepper into the sink one by one and sifted through them. Other than some little black insects I found nothing. The stove was an old gas stove. I took up the grillwork over the burners, looked carefully at the oven. The stove couldn't be moved without disconnecting the gas pipe. I was willing to bet Cathy Connelly never had. I took all the pans out of the under sink cabinet, and wormed under the sink on my back, using my flashlight to examine it all. A cockroach. There was little food in the old gas refrigerator. I emptied it. A couple of TV dinners. I melted them under the hot water in the sink and found nothing. I took the panel off of the bottom and looked carefully in. The motor was thick with dust kitties, and the drip pan was gummy with God knows what.

The living room was of course the one that took time. It was about two in the morning when I found something. In the bottom bureau drawer was a cigar box containing letters, bills, canceled checks. I took it over to the day bed, sat down, and began to read through them. There were two letters from her mother full of aimless amenities that made my throat tighten. The dog got on the school bus and her father had gotten a call from the school and had to leave the store and go get it, younger brother was in a junior high school pageant, momma had lost three pounds, she hoped Cathy was watching what she ate, daddy sent his love.

The third letter was different. It was on the stationery of a Peabody motel. It said:

Darling,
You are beautiful when you are asleep. As I write this I am looking at you and the covers are half off you so I can see your breasts. They are beautiful. I want to climb back into bed with you, but I must leave. You can cut my eight o'clock class, but I can't. I won't mark you absent though and I'll be thinking about last night all the time. The room is paid for and you have to leave by noon, they said. I love you.

There was no date, no signature. It was written in a distinctive cursive script.

For crissake! A clue. A goddamned clue. I folded the note up and put it in my inside coat pocket. So far I was guilty of breaking and entering, possession of burglar's tools, and destruction of property. I figured tampering with evidence would round things out nicely. I wanted to run right out and track down my clue, but I didn't. I searched the rest of the room. There were no other clues.

I turned off the lights, moved the chair, and went out. The door wouldn't stay shut because of the broken padlock. I went out the front way this time, as if I belonged. When I got to my car I put the pinch bar back in the trunk, got in the car, and sat for a bit. Now that I had a clue, what exactly was I supposed to do with it? I looked at my watch, 3 A.M. Searching apartments is slow business. I turned on the interior light in my car, took out my clue, and read it again. It said the same thing it said the first time. I folded it up again and tapped my front teeth with it for about fifteen seconds. Then I put it back in my pocket, turned off the interior light, started up the car, and went home. When I decide something I don't hesitate.

I went to bed and dreamed I was a miner and the tunnel was collapsing and everyone else had left. I woke up with the dream unfinished and my clock said ten minutes of seven. I looked at the bureau. My clue was up there where

I'd left it, partly unfolded, along with my loose change and my jackknife and my wallet. Maybe I'd catch somebody today. Maybe I'd detect something. Maybe I'd solve a crime. There are such days. I'd even had some. I climbed out of bed and plodded to the shower. I hadn't worked out in four days and felt it. If I solved something this morning, maybe I could take the afternoon off and go over to the Y.

I took a shower and shaved and dressed and went out. It was only 7:45 and cold. The snow was hard-crusted and the sun glistened off it very brightly. I put on my sunglasses. Even through their dark lenses it was a bright and lovely day. I stopped at a diner and had two cups of coffee and three plain doughnuts. I looked at my watch, 8:15. The trouble with being up and at 'em bright and early was once you were up most of the 'em that you wanted to be at weren't out yet.

I bought a paper and cruised over to the university. There was room to park in a tow zone near the gymnasium. I parked there and read the paper for half an hour. Nowhere was there mention of the fact that I'd found a clue. In fact nowhere was anyone even predicting that I would. At nine o'clock I got out and went looking for Iris Milford.

She wasn't in the newspaper office. The kid cropping photos at the next desk told me she never came in until the afternoon, and showed me her class schedule pasted on the corner of her desk. With his help, I figured out that from nine to ten she had a sociology course in room 218 of the chemistry building. He told me how to get there. I had a half-hour wait in the corridor, where I entertained myself examining the girl students who went by. During class time they were sparse and I had nothing else to do but marvel at the consistency with which the university architects had designed their buildings. Cinder block and vinyl tile seem to suffice for all seasons. At ten minutes to ten the bell rang and the kids poured into the corridor. Iris saw me as she came out of the classroom. She said, "Hell, Spenser. How'd you know where to find me?"

I said, "I'm a trained detective. Want some coffee?"

We went to the cafeteria in the student union. Above the cafeteria entrance someone had scrawled in purple magic marker, "Abandon All Hope Ye Who Enter Here."

I said, "Isn't that from Dante?"

She said, "Very good. It's written over the entrance to hell in book three of *The Inferno*."

I said, "Aw, I bet you looked that up."

The cafeteria was modernistic as far as cinder block and vinyl tile will permit. The service area along one side was low-ceilinged and close. The dining area was three stories high, with one wall of windows that reached the ceiling and opened on a parking lot. The cluttered tables were a spectrum of bright pastels and the floor was red quarry tile in squares. It was somewhere between an aviary and Penn Station. It was noisy and hot. The smoke of thousands of cigarettes drifted through the shafts of winter sunlight that fused in through the windows. Abandon All Hope Ye Who Enter Here.

I said, "Many campus romances start here?"

She laughed and shook her head. "Not hardly," she said. "You want to scuff hand and hand through fallen leaves, you don't go here."

We stood in line for our coffee. The service was cardboard, by Dixie. I paid, and we found a table. It was cluttered with paper plates, plastic forks, and cardboard beverage trays and napkins. I crumpled them together and deposited them in a trash can.

"How long you had this neatness fetish?" Iris asked.

I grinned, took a sip of coffee.

"You find Cathy Connelly?" she asked.

"Yeah," I said, "but she was dead."

131

Iris's mouth pulled back in a grimace and she said, "Shit."

"She'd been drowned in her bathtub, by someone who tried to make it look accidental."

Iris sipped her coffee and said nothing.

I took the letter from my inside pocket and gave it to her. "I found this in her room," I said.

Iris read it slowly.

"Well, she didn't die a virgin," Iris said.

"There's that," I said.

"She was sleeping with some professor," Iris said.

"Yep."

"If you can find out what eight o'cock classes she had, you'll know who."

"Yep."

"But you can't get that information because you've been banished from the campus."

"Yep."

"Which leaves old Iris to do it, right?"

"Right."

"Why do you want to know?"

"Because I don't know. It's a clue. There's a professor in here someplace. The missing manuscript would suggest a professor. Terry says she heard Powell talking to a professor before he was killed, now Cathy Connelly appears to have been sleeping with a professor, and she's dead. I want to know who he is. He could be the same professor. Can you get her class schedule?"

"This year?"

"All years, there's no date on the note."

"Okay, I got a friend in the registrar's office. She'll check it for me."

"How soon?"

"As soon as she can. Probably know tomorrow."

"I'm betting on Hayden," I said.

"As a secret lover?"

"Yep. The manuscript is medieval. He's a medieval specialist. He teaches Chaucer, which is an early class. Terry Orchard was up early for her Chaucer course the day that Powell threatened some professor on the phone. The conversation implied that the professor on the phone had an early class. Hayden pretended not to know Terry Orchard when in fact he did know her. He's a raging radical according to a very reliable witness. There's enough coincidence for me to wager on. Why don't you get in touch with your friend and find out if I'm right?"

She said, "Soon as I finish my coffee. I'll call you when I know."

I left her and headed back for my car.

I was right. Iris called me at eleven-thirty the next morning to report that Cathy Connelly had taken Chaucer this year with Lowell Hayden at eight o'clock Monday, Wednesday, and Friday. The only other eight o'clock class she'd had in her three years at the university had been a course in Western civilization taught by a woman.

"Unless she was gay," Iris said, "it looks like Dr. Hayden."

"You took the same course, right?" I asked.

"Yeah."

"Got any term papers or exams, or something with a sample of his writing?"

"I think so. Come on over to the newspaper office. I'll dig some up."

"Don't you ever go to class?"

"Not while I'm tracking down a criminal, I don't."

"I'll be over," I said.

When I got there Iris had a typewritten paper bound in red plastic lying on her desk. It was twenty-two pages long and titled "The Radix Trait: A Study of Chaucer's Technique of Characterization in *The Canterbury Tales*." Underneath it said "Iris Milford," and in the upper right hand corner it said "En 308, Dr. Hayden, 10/28." Above the title in red pencil with a circle around it was the grade A—.

"Inside back page," she said. "That's where he comments."

I opened the manuscript. In the same red pencil Hayden

had written, "Good study, perhaps a bit too dependent on secondary sources, but well stated and judicious. I wish you had not eschewed the political and class implications of the *Tales*, however."

I took the note out of my coat pocket and put it down beside the paper. It was the same fancy hand.

"Can I have this paper?" I asked Iris.

"Sure, why, want to read it in bed?"

"No, I'm housebreaking a puppy."

She laughed. "Take it away," she said.

Near my office there was a Xerox copy center. I went in and made a copy of the note and the comment page in Iris's paper. I took the original up to my office and locked it in the top drawer of my desk. I put the copies in my pocket and drove over to see Lowell Hayden.

He wasn't in his office, and the schedule card posted on his door indicated that he had no more classes until Monday. Across the street at a drugstore I looked for his name in the directory. He wasn't listed in the Boston books. I looked up the English Department and called them.

"Hi," I said, "this is Dr. Porter. I'm lecturing over here at Tufts this evening and I'm trying to locate Lowell Hayden. We were grad students together. Do you have his home address?"

They did, and they gave it to me. He lived in Marblehead. I looked at my watch, 11:10. I could get there for lunch.

Marblehead is north, through the Callahan Tunnel and along route 1A. An ocean town, yachting center, summer home, and old downtown district that reeked of tar and salt and quaint. Hayden had an apartment in a converted warehouse that fronted on the harbor. First floor, front.

A big hatchet-faced woman in her midthirties answered my ring. She was taller than I am and her blond hair was pulled back in a tight bun. She wore no make-up, and the only thing that ornamented her face were huge Gloria

Steinem glasses with gold rims and pink lenses. Her lips were thin, her face very pale. She wore a man's green pullover sweater, Levis, and penny loafers without socks. Big as she was, there was no extra weight. She was as lean and hard as a canoe paddle, and nearly as sexy.

"Mrs. Hayden?" I asked.

"Yes."

"Is Dr. Hayden in?"

"He's in his study. What do you want?"

"I'd like to speak with him, please."

"He always spends two hours a day in his study. I don't permit him to be bothered during that time. Tell me what you want."

"You're beautiful when you're angry," I said.

"What do you want?"

I offered her my card. "If you'll give that to Dr. Hayden, perhaps he'll break his rules just once."

"I will do nothing of the kind," she said, without taking the card.

"Okay, but if you'll give him this card when he is through his meditations I'll be waiting out in my car, looking at the ocean, thinking long thoughts." I wrote on the back of the card, "Cathy Connelly?" and put the card down on the edge of the umbrella stand by the door. She didn't slam it but she closed it firmly. I had the feeling she did everything firmly.

I went back to my car and watched the sun glint on the water. There weren't many boats in the harbor in winter, mostly sea gulls, bobbing on the cold water and swooping in the bright sky. A lobster boat came slowly into the harbor mouth past the lighthouse on the point of Marblehead Neck. Behind me, the seafood restaurant on the wharf was filling with lunch time customers, and ahead of me two tourists were taking pictures of the wharf building. I watched the Hayden apartment. Hatchet face never so much as peeked out a window at me. Her husband as far as I could tell continued to meditate. The waves hit the wharf regularly; the interval between waves was about three seconds. After two hours and twenty minutes Lowell Hayden appeared at the front door and looked hard at me. I waved. He shut the door and I sat some more. Another half-hour and Hayden appeared again, this time wearing a tan poplin jacket with a fur-lined hood. Other than that he seemed to be dressed just as he had been the last time I saw him. His wife loomed behind him, much taller. She stood in the open door while he came to the car. Making sure I wouldn't mug him, I guess. He opened the door and got in. I smiled pleasingly.

He said, "Spenser, you'd better leave me alone." His little pale face was clenched and there was a flush on each cheekbone. He looked a bit like Raggedy Andy.

"Why is that?" I said.

"Because you'll get hurt."

"No," I said. "You're not saying it right. Keep the lips almost motionless, and squinch your eyes up."

"I'm warning you now, Spenser. You stay away from me. I have friends who know how to deal with people like you."

"You gonna call in some hard cases from the Modern Language Association?"

"I mean people who will kill you if I say so."

"Oh, Mrs. Hayden, you mean."

"You leave her out of this. You've upset her enough." He looked nervously at the motionless and implacable figure in the doorway.

"She asking you funny questions about Cathy Connelly?"

"I don't know anything about Cathy Connelly."

"Yeah, you do," I said. "You know about spending the night with her in a motel in romantic Peabody. You know that she's dead, and you now how she died."

"I do not." His resonant voice was up about three

137

octaves; for the first time it matched his appearance. He glanced back at the woman in the doorway. "I'll have you killed, you bastard. I don't know anything about this. You leave me alone or you'll be so sorry you can't imagine."

"You don't really think Joe Broz will kill me on your say-so, do you?"

His pale face went chalk white. The flush left his cheeks and his left eyelid began to flutter. My right hand was resting on the steering wheel and he suddenly dug his fingernails into it. I yanked my hand away and Hayden jumped out of the car and walked very fast to the house.

"You'll see," he shouted back at me. "You'll see, you bastard. You'll see."

He went in past his wife, who closed the door. Firmly.

There were four red scratches on the back of my hand. Lucky it wasn't the wife; they would have been on my throat. I leaned back in the car and took a big lungful of air and let it out slowly. I knew something. I knew that Hayden was it, or at least part of it. He'd overreacted. And he'd made a big mistake to threaten me with tough-guy connections. It had to be Broz, and his reaction to the name made it certain. English professors don't know hired muscle unless there's something funny. Here there was something very funny. But exactly what? What was Lowell Hayden's connection with Joe Broz? What did either one have that the other would want? Hayden didn't have money, which was all Broz would want. The connection had to be dope somewhere. Powell was reputed to be a contact for heroin. Powell might be connected with Hayden. Hayden was connected to Cathy Connelly, who was connected to Terry Orchard, who was connected to Powell.

My head began to feel like a mare's nest. I could connect Hayden to Cathy Connelly for sure. The rest was just speculation and what I knew in my gut wasn't going to get Terry Orchard out of jail. My best hope was Hayden's hysteria. He panicked pretty easily and if I kept pushing at him who knows what else might boil to the surface? But first I needed another point of view, a third party you might say. It was time to go call on old Mark Tabor again. And this time maybe I'd stay longer and lean a little heavier.

• 18 •

Mark Tabor was not home when I got to Westland Avenue. I had to walk up four flights of stairs to find that out. I walked back down and sat outside in my car. I spent a lot of time doing that. It was getting dark and colder; I kept the motor running and the heater going. My stomach was making great cavernous noises at 6:30 when Tabor showed up. He came down from Mass Ave with his hands deep in the pockets of a pea jacket, the collar up, and his red corona of hair blossoming about the dark coat like an eruption. He turned in at his building and I came up behind him, reaching his door as he was closing it. I hit it hard with my shoulder and it flew open, propelling Tabor across the room. He tripped over the bed as he staggered backward and fell on it. I shut the door hard behind me, for effect. I wanted him scared.

"Hey, man, what the hell," he said.

"The hell is this, stupid," I said. "If you don't answer what I ask I'm going to pound you into an omelet."

"Who the Christ are you, man?"

"My name's Spenser, I was here before, and you proved too tough for me to break. I'm back for another try, boy, only this time I'll try harder."

"I don't know nothing you care about, man."

"Oh yeah, you do. You know about Lowell Hayden. Tell me. Tell me everything you know about Lowell Hayden."

"Hey, man, all I know he's a professor, you know. That's all I know."

140

"No, you know more than that. You know he's in SCACE with you, don't you?" I moved toward him and he scrambled off the bed and backed toward the wall.

"No, man, honest . . ."

"Yeah, you know that. And you'll tell me. But there's something else."

I was on his side of the bed now and close to him. He tried to jump onto the bed and away from me. I grabbed him by the shirtfront and slammed him back up against the wall.

"Before you tell me about Hayden, I want to speak to you about the manner in which you address me."

I had my face very close to his, and was holding him very tight up against the wall. "I want you to address me as Mr. Spenser. I do not want you to address me as 'man.' Do you understand that?"

"Aw, man . . ." he began, and I slapped him in the face.

"Mr. Spenser, boy," I said.

"Lemme go, Mr. Spenser. You got no right to come in here and hassle me."

I jerked him away from the wall and slammed him back up against it.

"We're not here to discuss my rights, stupid, we're here to talk about Lowell Hayden. Is he in SCACE?"

"No, man . . . Mr. Spenser."

I slapped him across the face again, a little harder, twice.

"I'll kill you if I have to, stupid," I said.

"Okay, okay, yeah he was in SCACE, but he was like a secret member, you know? Dennis Powell brought him in; he said this dude would be like a faculty contact only under cover, you dig? And me and Dennis would be like the only ones to know." He was beginning to sniffle a little as he talked.

"And the manuscript, what about that?" I twisted a

141

little more shirtfront up in my hand and lifted him up on tiptoe for emphasis.

"I didn't have nothing to do with that; that was Dennis and Hayden. Hayden arranged it. I never even saw it."

"Okay, one more, was Powell dealing hard drugs on campus?"

"Yeah."

"What?"

"Skag, mostly."

"Where did he get it?"

"I don't know."

I slammed him against the wall again.

"Honest to God, Mr. Spenser, I don't know. Ask Hayden, him and Dennis were close as a bastard. He might know, I don't know."

"How did Dennis get killed?"

"I don't know."

"How did Cathy Connelly get killed?"

"I don't know, honest to Christ, I don't know about any of that."

He was shaking and his teeth chattered.

I believed him. But I had some hard facts for the first time. I had Hayden connected with Powell. I had Powell connected with heroin, which meant mob connections. If Powell and Hayden were that close, I had Hayden connected to the mob. I had Hayden and Powell both connected to the Godwulf Manuscript and I had the Godwulf Manuscript connected to Broz. More than that I had Cathy Connelly connected to both Hayden and Terry Orchard. In fact, I had Hayden connected with two murders.

"Let me go, Mr. Spenser. I don't know anything else."

I realized I was still holding Tabor half off the ground. I let him go. He sank onto the bed and began to cry.

I said, "Everyone gets scared when they are overmatched in the dark; it's not something to be ashamed of, kid.''

He didn't stop crying and I couldn't think of anything else to say. So I left. I had a lot of information, but I had an unpleasant taste in my mouth. Maybe on the way home I could stop and rough up a Girl Scout.

It was raining when I came out, a cold rain about a degree above snow, and in the dark the wetness made the city look better than it was. The light diffused and reflected off things that in the daylight were dull and ugly.

It was nearly eight o'clock. I hadn't eaten since breakfast. I went to a steak house and ate. Halfway through my steak I caught sight of myself in the mirror behind the bar. I looked like someone who ought to eat alone. I didn't look in the mirror again.

It was twenty minutes of ten as I parked in front of my apartment. In front of me was parked an aggressively nondescript car made noticeable by the big whip antenna folded forward over the roof and clipped down. It was Quirk.

When I got out of the car he was waiting for me and I said, ''What the hell do you want, Lieutenant?''

''I want to talk with you. Let's go inside.''

Quirk was great for small talk. When we got to my apartment I offered him a drink. He said, ''Thanks.''

''Okay, Lieutenant, what do you want to talk about? How poor Cathy Connelly fell in the bathtub and hit her little head?''

''What have you got?'' Quirk said.

''What do you mean what have I got? You taking a survey for HEW?''

''What have you got on the Connelly thing and on Lowell Hayden and the Powell murder?''

''Say, you must be some kind of investigator; you know all about what I'm up to.''

Quirk stood up, walked across the room, and looked out my window. He took a long pull at the bourbon and water in his hand and turned around and looked at me.

"I'm trying, Spenser, I'm trying to ask you polite, and treat you like you weren't a wiseass sonova bitch, because I owe you. Because maybe I need you to do some stuff for me. Why don't you try to help me through this by trying out your nightclub act on someone else? What have you got for me?"

Quirk was right. I felt lousy about Mark Tabor and I was taking it out on Quirk. "I got three categories of things," I said. "What I know and can prove; what I know and can't prove; and what I don't know."

Quirk sat in my armchair and looked at me and listened.

"Here's what I know and can prove. Lowell Hayden and Cathy Connelly were lovers. They spent at least one night together in a Holiday Inn in Peabody—Peabody, what a romantic!—and I've got a note he wrote her that locks him up on that one. Lowell Hayden and Dennis Powell were in on the theft of the Godwulf Manuscript. Hayden was an anonymous member of a student radical group called SCACE. Powell was dealing heroin. I've got a witness that will confirm that. I told Joe Broz I'd stop messing around with the case if the manuscript were returned. The next day it was returned."

"But you're still messing around," Quirk said.

"Yeah," I said, "I lied."

"Broz probably won't like that."

"Probably won't," I said.

"What else can you prove?"

"Nothing. But here's what I know anyway. Hayden is tied to Broz. It was after I talked to him the first time that Broz warned me off. This afternoon when I talked to him he said he had people who would kill me if he said so. You and I know where to find people like that, but your average teacher of medieval lit doesn't. If Powell was dealing

heroin he was tied to the mob, too. That's too big a
coincidence that Powell and Hayden should both be mob
connected and connected to each other and not have it
mean something. Hayden had to have something to do
with drug pushing. That's the only thing that Broz would
have in common with a university community. More
connection: Hayden's girl friend was a roommate of
Powell's girl friend, Cathy Connelly and Terry Orchard,
and if Terry's story is true it would be Cathy Connelly who
would have known that Terry had a gun, and where she
kept it, and how to get it. If Terry's story is true, the killing
of Powell was not amateur work. Now who would have
both professional connections and access to knowledge of
Terry's gun?''

Quirk said, ''Hayden.''

''And,'' I said, ''the killing of Cathy Connelly was an
amateur production, even though Yates seemed to like it.
Powell was dead and Terry was in Charles Street at the
time. Of this interlocking quartet who does that leave?''

''Hayden.''

''Clues must be your game, Lieutenant,'' I said.
''You're two for two.''

''Got some more?''

''Yeah, here's the hard stuff. Why did Powell get
killed? Why did Terry get framed? Why did Cathy Connelly get killed? One point—Hayden is not playing with
fifty-two cards. I talked to him today, there're pieces
missing. Kidnaping that manuscript sounds just about
right for him. So if he's it in this game, it may be harder to
explain because he is not normal. The reasons he would do
things are not predictable reasons.''

''You got a nice assortment of possibilities,'' Quirk
said. ''So far you're into organized crime, dope pushing,
theft, radical politics, adultery, and murder. I'm not saying I agree with you. But if I did, Hayden would look good
to me. He would be the handle and I'd keep turning it until

something opened." Quirk stood up. "If you're messing with Joe Broz you might turn up dead some morning. I'd better know the name of this witness in case you do."

"Tabor," I said. "Mark Tabor, seventy-seven Westland Ave, Apartment forty-one."

"Thanks," Quirk said. "Thanks for the drink, too. See you."

I let him out. He was clearly sick with worry about me getting killed.

The next morning I went over to the university and put a tail on Hayden. I couldn't think of anything else to do. I knew he was involved in two killings and that Terry was involved in none, but I couldn't prove it. I could nail him for manuscript-naping or whatever, but I was willing to bet that the university wouldn't press charges, and even if they did, with a good lawyer and a first offense what would happen to him? I could threaten to tell his wife about Cathy Connelly, but he wasn't likely to confess to murder to placate his wife. But he knew I knew and it had to bother him. He might do something stupid, and if I kept after him I might catch him doing it.

So in the fresh of morning when Hayden showed up for his nine o'clock class in pre-Shakespearean drama I was lurking about the north end of the corridor and when he came out fifty minutes later, I was at the south end of the corridor getting a drink from the bubbler. While he conferred with students in his office about image patterns in *The Play of the Weather* and *Gammer Gurton's Needle*, I studied the announcements and grad school advertisements on the bulletin board down the corridor.

Surveillance on a guy that knows you is hard, and it's much harder when you're trying to do it alone. In the long run it's not possible. Eventually Hayden would catch me and there was nothing to do about it. On the other hand, before he did I might catch him, and anyway, I didn't know what else to do.

Hayden ate lunch in his office from a brown paper bag and a thermos. I didn't. By three o'clock that afternoon I was pretty sure how Hayden would spot me. He'd hear my stomach rolling. At four Hayden went to his *Beowulf* class. As soon as he was safely into his lecture, I ducked out, and bought half a dozen hamburgers at McDonald's. On the way back I bought a pint of Wild Turkey bourbon at a package store and was back in time to pick Hayden up after class and follow him to the parking lot.

Following him through the rush hour traffic was two-handed work and I didn't get to my supper until we were through the Callahan Tunnel and into East Boston. By the time we got to Lynn Shore Drive I'd eaten three cold hamburgers and swallowed about two inches of the pint. A cold McDonald's hamburger is halfway between a jelly doughnut and a hockey puck, but the nine-dollar bourbon helped.

I sat at the head of Hayden's street with the motor idling and the heater on until nine o'clock, when I ran low on gas and had to shut off the motor. By ten-fifteen I was cold. The hamburgers were long gone, though the memory lingered on the back of my throat, and I was almost through the bourbon. During that time Hayden had not come to me and confessed. He had not had a visit from Joe Broz or Phil, or the Ghost of Christmas Future. The Ceremony of Moloch had not shown up and sung "The Sweetheart of Sigma Chi" under his window. At eleven o'clock the lights in his living room went out and I went home—stiff, sore, tired, crabby, dyspeptic, cold, and about five-eighths drunk.

The next day we did it all again. This time I brought along a satchel of sandwiches and a large thermos of coffee. At the end of the day my stomach felt better, but I didn't know anything more and I had discovered new dimensions of boredom.

On the third day things picked up. It was raining again.

Hard and steady. Everything was frosted with slush. Hayden had a class from four to five and it was dark when I stood in a doorway across the street and watched him get in his car in the parking lot. He was turning over the engine when two guys got in with him. One in front, one in back. The windshield wipers went on, then the headlights. The car began to back out of its space. My car was parked on a hydrant one hundred feet from the doorway and I was in it with the motor running when Hayden's car turned out of the parking lot. I stayed close behind him. Too close really, but it was dark and wet and I was worried. The two guys that got in his car didn't look like poets to me and I didn't want to lose Hayden. He was all I had, and if something became of him, nothing much good would become of Terry Orchard.

We turned south on Huntington Avenue, past the new high-rise apartments, a hospital, another college, and out onto the Jamaicaway. Big houses, mostly brick, set well back and sumptuous, lined the road. Elms which had survived the Dutch disease arched over it, and to the right in an extended hollow was Jamaica Pond, wooded and grassy under the gray slush. Hayden's car pulled off the road and parked on the shoulder. I drove on by, turned left into a side street beyond, and parked.

I cut through the back yard of a large brick Dutch colonial house on the corner and came out opposite where Hayden's car was parked on the shoulder across the street. I didn't see any of them. The hard rain and warm weather were causing the wet slush to steam and a fog to rise from the rotting ice on the pond. I ran across the street and came up behind Hayden's car. It was empty. I realized that I had my gun in my hand though I didn't recall taking it from the hip holster. I stopped and listened. No sound but the rain and the cars on the Jamaicaway whooshing past on their way to Dedham and Milton. My stomach buzzed with tension.

There were tracks in the slush leading down toward the pond. I followed them into the mist. Closer to the pond it was so dense I could only see a few feet ahead.

I half expected to see Beowulf jump out of the bog and rip the arm off something . . . "My God, Holmes, those are the footprints of a gigantic hound . . ." I was wearing a hip-length wool jacket and the rain was soaking through along my shoulders. The wet wool smelled like a grammar school coatroom. Ahead of me I heard a kind of low wail. I stopped still in the dark. In front of me there were indistinct figures. I looked at them obliquely as I'd learned to do a long time ago in Korea, and they came into sharper focus. Hayden was the one making the mournful noise. He seemed to be having trouble standing and one of the other men had him under the arms. He stepped away and Hayden slumped to his knees and began to wail louder. The man who hadn't been holding him brought a long-barreled pistol from his side and placed it against the back of Hayden's head. I turned sideways as you do on the pistol range, and yelled, "Freeze!"

The guy with the gun snapped around and I felt the thump in my side simultaneous to the muzzle flash and before I heard the shot. It felt like I'd been hit in the ribs with a brick. I staggered, steadied myself, let out my breath, and brough my gun down on the middle of his chest . . . slack . . . squeeze . . . and my own shot exploded. He fell over backward. His buddy was shooting now and a bullet thunked into a tree beside me. Out of the edge of my vision I saw Hayden crawling for some bushes. I ducked behind the tree. There was no pain yet but my whole left side was numb and I felt a little dizzy. It was quiet again. Up on the Jamaicaway the headlights were fuzzy in the fog and the whoosh of their passage was cottony. The rain droned down. I slid down the tree and stretched out, belly down in the slush, and peered around

150

the edge of the tree. I couldn't see anyone. Still on my belly I began to inch backward.

About ten feet in back of the tree was a big old blue spruce whose bottom boughs skirted out six or eight feet around the bottom. I inched backward under them and lay still. Nothing moved. I was feeling dizzier and the first twiches of hurt were cutting through the numbness in my side. The slush was cold and underneath the tree the earth had started to thaw and turn to mud. Inching backward for ten feet had scraped a lot of it up under my coat.

I wondered if I'd die here. Face down under a spruce tree in the mud trying to keep a double murderer from getting shot by two hired thugs. I felt like I wanted to throw up. The noise would locate me. I swallowed it back. More silence while I fought the nausea and the cold.

After what seemed to be the duration of the Christian epoch I saw him. He had circled the tree where I'd first hidden and stepped out so that had I still been there he'd have been behind me. He was good; it took him maybe a second to realize I wasn't there and where I probably was. He spun and I put three shots into his chest, holding the gun in both hands to keep it steady. His gun bounced out of his hand and plopped softly into the slush. He fell more slowly sideways and joined it. I crawled out from under the tree and over to him. I felt in his neck for the big pulse. There wasn't any. I crawled on over to his buddy. Same thing. I got up and looked around for Hayden. I didn't see him and getting up was an error. My head spun and I sat down backward. The jar of it set the pain in my side to moving.

"Hayden," I yelled. No sound.

"Hayden, you dumb sonova bitch, it's Spenser. You're all right. They're dead. Come on out."

I got hunched over on one hip and put my gun back in

the holster. Then I got both hands onto the trunk of a sapling and pulled myself up.

"Hayden!"

He appeared from behind the bushes. His glasses were gone and his wet lank hair was plastered down over his small skull.

"They were going to kill me," he said. "They were going to kill me. They . . . they had no right . . ."

"Hayden, I been shot. I need help."

Hayden looked at me blankly. His eyes were red and swollen and his face, without glasses, looked naked.

"They were supposed to kill you," he said.

"Yeah, we'll talk about that, but gimme a hand."

The numbness was about gone now and the blood was a warm and sticky layer over the pain.

"We were allies. We were working together. And they were going to kill me."

He backed away from me, up toward the road. I let go of the tree and took a step toward him. He backed up faster.

"They were supposed to kill you."

I took another step toward him and fell down. He was now backing up so fast he was running. Like a corner back trying to stay with a wide receiver.

"Hayden!" I yelled.

He turned and ran up toward his car. Sonova bitch. At least he didn't kick me when I fell. I heard his car start but I didn't see him pull away. I was busy with other things. Two more tries convinced me that I'd have trouble walking up the hill, so I crawled. It was getting harder as the dizziness and the nausea progressed.

• 20 •

I don't know how long it took me to get up that hill to the street. Every few feet I had to rest and the last hundred feet of so I had to drag myself along on my stomach. I pulled myself over the curb and rested with my cheek in the gutter of the road and the rain drumming on my back. The pain drummed even harder in my side and there was a kind of counterpoint throb in my head. Then, suddenly, there was a big red-faced MDC cop standing over me in the glare of headlights and the steady pulse of the blue light. I didn't know how long I'd been out or where I was exactly.

"Just lay there, Jack, don't move around."

"I'm not drunk," I said.

"I can tell that, Jack. The left side of your coat is soaked with blood."

"I'm not drunk," I said again. It seemed very important to keep saying it. At the same time I knew he knew I wasn't drunk. He'd just said that he knew that. "I'm not," I said. The cop nodded. His face was red and healthy looking. He had a thick lower lip and a fine gray stubble on his chin. His partner brought the folding stretcher and they inched me onto it.

"Jesus Christ," I said.

Then I was looking up at the funny big light that diffuses the glare and the tubes and apparatus and a woman in a white coat, and I realized my coat and shirt were off.

"I been shot," I said.

"That was my diagnosis too." She was bending over and looking at my side closely.

"Bullet went right through, banged off a rib, probably cracked it—I don't think it's broken—and went on out. Tore up the latissimus dorsi a bit, caused a lot of blood loss and some shock. You'll live. This will sting." She swabbed something on the wound.

"Jesus Christ," I said.

A nurse wheeled me on the table down to have the rib x-rayed. Then she wheeled me back. The same ruddy-faced MDC cop that had picked me up was sitting on one of the other treatment tables in the cubicle off the emergency room. His partner leaned against the door jamb. He was skinny with pimples.

"I'll need a statement," Ruddy-face said.

"Yeah, I imagine. Look, you know Quirk, homicide commander?"

He nodded.

"Call him, tell him I'm here and need to see him. He'll come down and I'll give the statement to both of you. You been through my wallet yet?"

"Yep."

"Okay, you know my name and my line of work. It's important that Quirk gets what I have to say. A guy might get killed and he's the key to a couple of murders."

The doctor returned with my x-rays and pushed past Pimples into the room. "As I said, rib cracked. I'll tape it and bandage the wound, then we'll put you to bed. In two or three days you'll be back on your feet."

Ruddy-face said to his partner, "Go call the lieutenant, Pooler."

Pooler said, "How come he gets special treatment? I say we get his statement and let Quirk know through channels."

"That's what you say, huh." Ruddy-face took out a big wooden kitchen match and stuck it in his mouth and chewed on it.

"Yeah, how come because the guy's got a private

154

license we have to kiss his a₋₋₋ Quirk'll get to his statement when he's ready.''

Ruddy-face took the match oᵤₜ of his mouth and examined the chewed end.

"You be sure and call the lieutenant by his last name when you see him, Pooler. He'll like that. Makes him feel he's popular with the men.''

"Jesus Christ . . .''

Ruddy-face got a very hard sound into his voice. "Goddammit, Pooler, will you call the lieutenant? This guy got shot, two other people got killed. Lieutenant's going to see him anyway. If he knows him maybe he'll want to see him sooner. Why would this guy make up the story? 'Cause he's queer for the lieutenant? If the guy's right and we don't call we'll be directing traffic in South Dorchester Christmas morning.''

Pooler went. The doctor was busy wrapping my rib cage and ignored them both.

"Where am I?'' I asked her. "Boston City?''

"Yep.''

When the doctor got through a nurse wheeled me up to a ward bed. The ruddy-faced cop came with me. His partner stayed down to wait for Quirk. The ward was half-empty and depressing.

"It'll be full by morning,'' the nurse said. She cranked up the bed and she and the cop slid me onto it.

"Doctor says give you a shot to help you sleep,'' she said.

"Not yet,'' I said. "Wait until I've talked with the cops.''

Ruddy-face nodded at her that he agreed.

"Okay,'' she said to Ruddy-face. "Tell the floor nurse when you're through and we'll come in and give him his shot then.'' She left. Ruddy-face sat down beside the bed.

"How you feel?'' he asked.

"Like I been kicked in the side by a giraffe,'' I said.

He fumbled inside his coat and brought out a pint of Old Overholt.

"Want a shot before the nurse gets back?" he said.

I took the bottle.

"Crank me up," I said. He raised the head end of the bed so I was half-sitting, and I inhaled half his bottle.

I handed him back the bottle. He wiped the top off with his hand in an unconscious gesture of long practice, and took a long pull. He handed it back to me.

"Finish it," he said. "I got another one in the car."

The liquor burned hot in my stomach and the pain was a little duller. Quirk arrived; Belson was with him. Quirk looked at the bottle and then at Ruddy-face. I put the bottle down empty on the night stand away from Ruddy-face.

"Where'd he get the bottle, Kenneally?"

Ruddy-face shrugged. "Must a had it with him, Lieutenant. How ya doing, Frank?"

Quirk said, "I'll bet." Belson nodded at Ruddy-face.

"Okay—" Quirk turned to me—"lemme have it."

Belson had a notebook out. Ruddy-face got up and moved to the end of the ward, where he broke out a new match and began to chew on it.

"I'm fine thanks, Lieutenant. Just a little old bullet wound."

"Yeah, good, let's hear it all. There's two carcasses downstairs right now that the MDC people brought in from Jamaica Pond. I want to hear."

I told him. He listened without interruption. When I got through he turned to Belson. "You see the two, Frank?"

"Yeah. One of them is a gopher for Joe Broz, Sully Roselli. I don't know the other one. His driver's license says Albert J. Brooks. Mean anything to you?"

Quirk shook his head and looked at me. I shook mine too.

"CID is looking into him," Belson said.

"Right, now see what you can do about getting a leash on Hayden. Pick up and hold."

"Yates will be disappointed," I said.

"Can't be helped," Quirk said. "Hayden's a witness to attempted murder and two homicides. Got to bring him in."

Quirk looked back at me, thoughtfully.

"Two of them in the dark," he said. "Not bad."

He nodded at Belson and they left. As they went out Quirk said to Kenneally, "Tell the nurse we're through. And don't give him any more booze."

By the time the nurse got there I was halfway under again and barely felt the needle jab.

21

I woke up in bright daylight, confused, to the sound of a monotonous deep cough from the other end of the room. I shifted in the bed and felt the pain in my side and remembered where I was. The coughing went on down the ward. I creaked myself around on the bed, dropped my legs over the side, and got myself sitting up. All the beds were full. I had a hospital johnny and an adhesive sash around my torso. Very natty. I stood up. My legs felt spongy and I braced myself with one hand against the bed. Steady. I walked the length of the bed. Not bad. I walked back to the head. Better. I U-turned, back toward the foot. Then I started down the length of the ward. Slow, shaky, but halfway down I didn't have to hold on. An old man with no teeth mumbled to me from one of the beds.

"You get hell if they catch you out of bed," he said.

"Watch," I said.

I kept going. All the way to the end of the ward, then back, then down the ward again. I was feeling balanced and ambulatory when the floor nurse came in. She had a cheerful Irish face and a broad beam. She looked at me as if I'd messed on the floor.

"Oh, no," she said. "Right back in the bed, there. We're not supposed to be strolling around. Come on."

"Cookie," I said, "we are doing more than strolling. We are getting the hell out of here as soon as we can find our pants."

"Nonsense, I want you to hop right back in that bed.

This minute." She clapped her hands sharply for emphasis.

"Don't do that," I said. "I may faint and you'll have to give me mouth-to-mouth resuscitation." I kept on walking.

She glanced at the name card at the foot of my empty bed. "Mr. Spenser, must I call the resident?"

In the middle of the ward was a large double door. I pushed it open. It was a walk-in closet with baskets on shelves. My clothes were in one of them. I put on my pants, still soggy with the mud half-dried on them.

"Mr. Spenser." She stood in semiparalysis in the doorway. I dropped the johnny and slipped my jacket on over the bandaged body. Shirt and underwear were so blood-soaked and mud-drenched that I didn't bother. I jammed my feet into my loafers. They had been my favorites, tassles over the instep. One tassle was now missing and there were two inches of mud caked all over them. My gun and wallet were missing. I'd worry about that later.

I pushed past the nurse, whose face had turned very red.

"Don't fret, cookie," I said. "You've done what you could, but I've got stuff I have to do and promises to keep. And for a guy with my virility what's a bullet wound or so?"

I kept going. She came behind me and at the desk outside by the elevator a second nurse joined her in protest. I ignored them, and went down the elevator.

When I got outside onto Harrison Ave it was a very nice day—sunny, pleasant, and it occurred to me that I didn't have a car or money or a ride home. I didn't have my watch either but it was early. There was little traffic on the streets. I turned back toward the hospital and my Irish nurse came out.

"Mr. Spenser, you're not in condition to walk out like this. You've lost blood; you've suffered shock."

"Listen to me now, lovey," I said. "You're probably

right. But I'm leaving anyway. And we both know you can't prevent it. But what you can do is lend me cab fare home.''

She looked at me startled for a minute and then laughed. ''Okay,'' she said. ''You deserve something for sheer balls. Let me get my purse.'' I waited, and she was back in a minute with a five-dollar bill.

''I'll return it,'' I said.

She just shook her head.

I walked over to Mass Avenue and waited till a cab cruised by. When I got in the cabby said, ''You got money?''

I showed him the five. He nodded. I gave him the address and we went home.

When he let me out I gave him the five and told him to keep it.

I got a look at my reflection in the glass door of my apartment building and I knew why he'd asked me for money first. My coat was black with mud, blood, and rain. The same for my pants. My ankles showed naked above the mud-crusted shoes. I had a forty-six-hour beard stubble and a big bruise on my forehead I must have gotten when I crawled over the curbstone the night before.

I realized I didn't have a key. I rang for the super. When he came he made no comment.

''I've lost my key,'' I said. ''Can you let me into my apartment?''

''Yep,'' he said and headed up the stairs to my place. I followed. He opened my door and I went in.

''Thanks,'' I said.

''Yep,'' he said. I closed the door.

I wondered if he'd noticed that I looked different. Maybe he thought it an improvement.

Despite the palpable silence of the place I was glad to be home. I looked at my pine Indian still on the sideboard in the living room. I hadn't gotten to the horse yet and he seemed to flow into a block of wood. I went into the kitchen, took off the coat, pants, and shoes, and stuffed them into the wastebasket. Then I went in and took a shower. I kept the wounded side away from the water as much as I could. I shaved with the shower still running and stepped back in to rinse off the shave cream. I toweled dry, and dressed. Gray, hard-finished slacks with a medium flare, blue paisley flowered shirt with short sleeves, blue wool socks, mahogany colored buckle boots with a side zipper, broad mahogany belt with a brass buckle. I liked getting dressed, feeling the clean cloth on my clean body. I paid special attention to it all. It was good not to be dead in the mud under a blue spruce tree.

In the kitchen I made coffee and put six homemade German sausages in the fry pan. They were big fat ones I had to go up to the North Shore to buy from a guy who made them in the back of the store. You should always start them on low in a cold fry pan. When they began to sizzle I cored a big green apple and peeled it. I sliced it thick, dipped the slices in flour, and fried them in the sausage fat. The coffee had perked and I had a cup with heavy cream and two sugars. The smell of the sausage and apple cooking began to make my throat ache. I slipped a spatula under the apples and turned them. I took the sausages out with tongs and let them drain on a paper towel. When the apple rings were done, I drained them with the sausages and ate both with two big slices of coarse rye bread and wild strawberry jam in a crock that you can buy up at the Mass Ave end of Newbury Street.

I listened to the morning news on the radio while I drank the last of my coffee. They mentioned the shooting in the Jamaicaway but gave no names. I was referred to as a Boston private detective. When it was over I switched off the radio, left the dishes where they were, and went to my bedroom. I got a spare gun out of the drawer and put it in an extra hip holster. The hip holster had slots for six extra bullets and I slipped them in and clipped it to my belt with the barrel end in my right back pocket.

I got five ten-dollar bills and a spare set of keys out of my top bureau drawer and slipped them into my pocket. Went to the front closet and got my other jacket. It was my weekend-in-the-country-jacket, cream-colored canvas with a sherpa lining that spilled out over the collar. I was saving it in case I was ever invited down to the Myopia Hunt Club for cocktails and a polo match. But since someone had shot a hole in my other coat I'd have to wear it now. It was 8:10 when I left my apartment. Smart, clean, well fed, and alive as a sonova bitch.

22

I took a cab back out to Jamaica Pond. My car was where I'd left it, keys still in the ignition, sunglasses still up on the dashboard. Hubcaps still on the wheels. Ah, law and order. I got in, started it up, and drove on back in town to my office. I opened all the windows, to air the place out, and checked my mail. Called the answering service to find that Marion Orchard had called three times and Roland Orchard once. I called Quirk to see if they'd found Hayden. They hadn't. I hung up and started to lean back in my chair and put my feet up. My side hurt and I froze in midmotion, remembering the wound, and eased my feet back to the ground. I sat very still for about thirty seconds, breathing in small shallow breaths till things subsided. Then I got up quite carefully and closed the window. No sudden moves.

It was time to start looking for Hayden. I looked down at Stuart Street; he wasn't there. I felt a good deal like going home and lying down on my bed, but Hayden probably wasn't there either. The best I could think of was go out and talk to Mrs. Hayden. As I was driving out to Marblehead again, the pain in my side began to be tiresome. At first it was almost a pleasant reminder that I was alive and hadn't bled to death in Jamaica Plain. But by now I was used to being alive and was again accepting it as my due, the common course of things, and the pain now served no other purpose than to remind me of my mortality. Also, the drive to Marblehead is among the worst in Massachusetts. It is only barely possible to reach

Marblehead from anywhere and the drive from Boston through the Callahan Tunnel, out Route 1A through East Boston, Revere, and Lynn is narrow, cluttered, ugly, and long. Particularly if you've recently been shot in the side.

There was a sea gull perched on the ridgepole of Hayden's gray weather duplex when I pulled in to the driveway. There was a larger number of people on the wharf than there had been last time, and I realized it was Saturday.

The shades of Hayden's place were drawn, but there was a stir of motion at the edge of one by the front door. I rang the bell and waited. No answer. No sound. I rang again. Same thing. I leaned on the bell and stayed there watching the ocean chop and flutter in the harbor and the bigger waves break against the causeway at the east end of the harbor. Inside I could hear the steady bleat of the bell. It sounded like a Bronx cheer. I felt it was directed at me—or was I getting paranoiac? She was tough; she hung in there for maybe five minutes. Then the door opened about two inches on a chain and she said, "Get out of here."

I said, "We've got to talk, Mrs. Hayden."

She said. "The police have been here already. I don't know where Lowell is. Get out of here."

I said, "Lowell's got one chance to stay alive, and I'm it. You shut the door on me and you'll be slamming the lid on your husband's casket."

The door slammed. Persuasive, that's me. Old silver tongue. I leaned on the bell some more. Another four or five minutes and she cracked. People who can endure bamboo slivers under the fingernails begin to weaken after ten minutes of doorbell ringing. She opened up again. Two inches, on the chain.

I said real quick, "Look. I saved your husband's life last night and got shot in the chest for my troubles and damn near bled to death because your husband ran off and left me. He owes me. You owe me. Let me save his life again. You won't get another chance." The door shut, but this time only for about thirty seconds. As I started to lean on the bell again I heard the chain bolt slide off and the door opened.

"Come in," she said.

She was as sumptuously dressed as she had been on my previous visit. This time it was brown corduroy pants that tapered at the ankles, brown leather sandals with a loop over the big toe, and a gray sweat shirt. Her hair was in the same tight bun, her face as empty of make-up as it had been. Her eyes behind the big pinkish eyeglasses were as warm and as deep as the end of a pool cue.

The apartment smelled of cat food. The front door opened into the living room. Beyond that I could see the kitchen and to the right of it a closed door, which I assume led to another room. Maybe the master's study. In front of me, opposite the door and along the right-hand wall, rose a staircase.

The living room was big and sunny and looked like the display window at Sid and Mabel's furniture outlet. There were four canvas director's chairs, two blue ones and two orange ones, more or less grouped around a clear plastic cube with an empty vase on it. On the far wall was a blond bookcase with a brilliant coat of shellac on it, which held an assortment of text-looking books, mostly paperbacks, and a pile on the bottom shelf of record albums and coarse-paper magazines without covers, which were probably academic journals. On top of it were a McIntosh amplifier, and a Garrard turntable. On each side, standing three feet high on the floor, two Fisher speakers. The whole rig probably had cost more than my car, and surely more than the furniture. On the floor were two rugs, fake fur in the shape they would have had were they real and skinned out to dry. One was a zebra, one a tiger. House beautiful.

"Sit down," she said and her thin lips barely moved as she talked. "Coffee?"

"Yes, please." I eased into one of the director's chairs. A fat Angora cat looked at me from the chair opposite, its yellow eyes as blank as doorknobs, its fur snarled and burry. It was the first time I could recall sitting in a director's chair. I had missed little, I decided. Mrs. Hayden appeared with the coffee in a white plastic mug, insulated, the kind you get with ten gallons of gas at an Exxon station. I took it black and sipped. It was instant.

"You say my husband needs your help. Why?"

"He's involved in one larceny and two murders. There is obviously a contract out on him. And if I don't find him before the contractors do he's going to have all his troubles solved for him with a neat lead injection."

"I don't know what you're talking about."

"I bet you do. But I'm not going to argue with you. I'm telling you that if he doesn't come in under cover, he's dead."

"What makes you think you can help him?"

"That's my line of work. I helped him last night. I can do it again. There's a homicide cop named Quirk who'll help too."

"Why should I trust you?"

"Because I got a hole in the right side of my body to prove it. Because you could trust me last night a hell of a lot more than I could trust your husband."

"Why do you care what happens to him?"

"I don't. But I care what happens to a twenty-year-old kid who'll end up in the women's reformatory unless I can find out the truth from your husband."

"And what happens to him when you find out whatever you think the truth is?"

"He'll live. I can't promise much else, but it's better than what he'll get if Broz gets there first. The Supreme Court has outlawed the death penalty, but Broz hasn't."

"This is ridiculous," she said in her flat thin voice. "I do not know anyone named Broz. I do not know anything about any killings or any girls going to jail. My husband is away for a few days on professional business."

She had her hands in her lap and was twisting the gold wedding ring round and round on her finger. I didn't say anything. Her voice went up half a note.

"It's absurd. You're absurd. It's an absurd fairy tale. My husband is a respected scholar. He is known all over America in his field. You wouldn't know that. You wouldn't know anything about us. You're nothing but a . . . a . . ."

"Cheap gumshoe?" I suggested.

"A snoop! A sneaky snoop! Nothing will happen to my husband. He's fine. He'll be back in a few days. He's just traveling professionally. I told you that. Why do you keep asking me?" Her voice went up another half note. "You bastard. Why are you hounding him? Why does everyone hound him? He's a scholar but you won't leave him alone. None of you. You, the police, those men, that girl . . ." Tears began to run down her face, her voice thickened.

"What girl?"

She wailed then. Her face got red and contorted and her mouth pulled back from her lips so that her gums were exposed. Her nose ran a little and she cried with her whole considerable frame—huge gasping sobs mixed with a high eerie sound like locusts. She drooled a bit too. I sipped on my coffee and said it again.

"What girl?"

Had she buried her face in her hands, or turned away, or fled the room it would have been tolerable. But she didn't. She sat, looking at me full face, and cried harder and harder till I began to think she would hurt herself. I couldn't keep looking. I got up and walked around the room. I looked out at the harbor. There was dust in random patterns on the windowpane. I put my hands in my pockets and walked back across the room and looked out the other window. She continued to howl. My side hurt and my head throbbed and I felt a little sick.

I looked at her sideways. She was trying to pick up her coffee cup but her hand shook so violently that the coffee sloshed out onto the coffee table and formed a brown puddle on the clear plastic. She kept trying, even though most of the coffee had sloshed out, and finally threw it frantically on the floor. The cat jumped off the chair and went into the kitchen.

She was screaming now steadily, except for the wrenching gasp when she had to breathe. I went over and put one hand on her shoulder. She jerked away and scrambled out of the chair. Both her hands were pushed out in front of her as she backed away from me, across the room. She stopped in the far corner and screamed with her hands straight out before her, palms up, as if pushing against something.

She swore at me now, the curses bubbling out through the screams as if her saliva were viscous, repetitious obscenities, including one I hadn't heard before. Then she stopped. The gasping breaths became more frequent, the screaming interludes shorter. Then she was whimpering. Then she was breathing as if she'd just run three miles, her chest heaving under the sweat shirt, her face wet with tears and sweat and saliva and nasal mucus. The effect of her hysteria had loosened her hair in strands and it stuck to the wetness on her cheek and forehead. She let her hands drop and straightened up in the corner. Her breathing slowed a little and the air ceased to rasp as it went to and from her lungs.

I said, "What girl?"

She shook her head without speaking. Then she went to the kitchen. I stepped to the kitchen door to make sure she didn't guillotine herself on the electric can opener, but her plan was better than that. She took a bottle of Scotch out of

168

one of the cabinets—they kept it in with the Wheaties—
removed the cap, and poured about half a cup into a water
glass. She didn't offer me any. She drank it as if it were a
nighttime cold medicine. All of it. And poured another.
This she carried back out into the living room and placed
before her on the glass cube as she sat back down. She
wiped her face with the sleeve of her sweat shirt, and
pushed her hair back off her face. From one pocket of the
corduroy Levis she took a bent packet of Kents. It took her
two matches to get a cigarette going. But she did it and
dragged a big lungful through the filter. The cigarette was
old and dry and the big drag consumed nearly half of it,
leaving a big glowing end which faded into ash and
dropped on the floor. She paid it no attention. What
looked like a descendant of the shaggy cat I'd seen earlier
appeared from the kitchen and mewed at the front door.
Mrs. Hayden seemed not to hear it. The cat mewed again
and I got up and let it out.

I turned back from the door and leaned against it with
my arms folded. My side didn't seem to hurt quite as much
if I stood that way.

"What about the girl?" I asked.

She shook her head.

"Look, Mrs. Hayden, you're in a box. You're got
trouble you can't handle. There are people trying to kill
your husband, the cops can't help because your husband is
involved in a criminal act, you don't know what to do, and
you just had hysterics to prove it. I'm all you've got. That
may not make you happy, but there isn't any way around
it. Asking your husband to go one-on-one with Joe Broz is
like putting a guppy in the piranha pool. If we don't find
him before Broz does he'll be eaten alive."

Maybe it was the "we." Maybe it was my impeccable
logic. Maybe it was desperation. But she said, "I'll take
you to him."

Like that. No preamble.

I said, "Okay."

She went to the hall closet and put on a red quilted ski parka with a hood and brown knitted woolen gloves with imitation leather palms. She stepped out of the sandals and stuck her bare feet into green rubber boots with yellow laces. They were all laced and ready to go. She put on a white and brown knitted ski cap with a yellow tassle on the top and we went.

In my car I said, "Where?"

She said, "Boston, the Copley Plaza." And she didn't say another thing all the way back into town.

23

The Copley Plaza fronts on Copley Square, as do the Boston Public Library and Trinity Church. In the center of the square is a sunken brick piazza where in the summer a fountain plays. It is very nice there and a classy area to hide out in. The hotel itself is high ceilinged and deep carpeted. At four each afternoon they serve tea in the lobby. And if you want a drink you can go to the Merry-Go-Round Room and sit at a bar that revolves slowly. There is a good deal of gilt and there are a good many Grecian Revival columns and the bellboys are very dignified in green uniforms with gold piping. I always felt I should lower my voice in the Copley Plaza, although my line of work didn't take me there with any regularity.

We went in the elevator, got off with another couple at the fourth floor, and walked down a corridor rather elegantly papered in pale beige. She knocked on the door of 411. The other couple passed us and went around the corner. They looked as if they might be on a honeymoon, or maybe they just worked in the same office and were on their lunch hour. Mrs. Hayden knocked again twice and then twice more. Christ, a secret code. Made you wish Ian Fleming had taken up music or something.

The door opened an inch on the chain. Hayden's voice emerged.

"What is it, Judy?" Judy? The name was bad; Mrs. Hayden wasn't a Judy. A Ruth, maybe, or an Elsie, but Judy?

"Let us in, Lowell."

"What's he doing here? Has he forced you, Judy? I told you never to bring anyone—"

Judy's voice got sharper. "Let us in, Lowell." And then more gently, "It's all right."

The door closed. The chain came off, and it opened again. In we went. It was a nice room with a big double bed, unmade now, and a window that looked out onto Dartmouth Street. The televison was tuned to a game show. The Boston *Globe* was scattered around the room.

Hayden shut the door, put the chain lock back on, and put the bed between me and him.

"What do you want?" he said.

The game show host introduced their defending champion, "Mrs. Tyler Moorehouse from Grand Island, Nebraska." The audience cheered. I reached over and shut it off.

I said, "You owe me a favor."

Judy Hayden went over around the bed and stood beside her husband. She was at least three inches taller.

"I don't owe you anything, Spenser. You just stay away from me."

He was a consistent sonova bitch.

"If I hadn't happened along last night, Hayden, you would now be enriching the soil in the area of Jamaica Pond. And if you don't help me now, that time will come again."

"They were supposed to kill you." He seemed to be repeating some kind of litany—by rote, as if, like ritual, the repetition of it, if done just right, would save him.

"They are not going to kill me, Hayden. They are going to kill you. Here's why. They want this case closed and forgotten. I keep nosing around in it and it is you that I've nosed up into the light. If they kill me that'll cause some more nosing around, by other people who know I'm nosing around you. You're the key, Hayden. You're the one who knows the stuff that Broz doesn't want known. If they kill me you are still the one who knows and you are still around and someone, like say a homicide cop named Quirk, might take hold of you and begin to shake you until what you know falls out. But—'' Mrs. Hayden had put an arm around her husband's shoulder, maternal—''but if they kill you there isn't anyone around who knows what Broz doesn't want known and Quirk and I can shake each other till we turn to butter and no information is going to fall out because we don't have it. How's that sound to you?''

Hayden just looked at me. I plowed ahead.

''I figure that you and Powell were involved in pushing dope at the university. Maybe for money, maybe because you wanted to turn on the sons of the middle class, maybe because you're a screwball and Tim Leary is your idol. Why doesn't matter so much for now; you can tell us that later. Broz supplied you. For him the university was a nice new market for some goods he had on hand and as long as you could deliver the market he could use you. But you and Powell had to get fancy. You stole that manuscript and held it for ransom. That was dumb, because that got the university police and me involved. No big threat, maybe, but there's no advantage to having legal types sniffing around. But what was dumber was that you and Powell had a falling out. About what, I don't know. You can tell me that, too. But it was you he was arguing with on the phone, and it was you who set him up for the mob hit. It had to be you because you're the only one around who could have supplied Terry Orchard's gun. You got it through Cathy Connelly.''

Judy Hayden's arm tightened around Hayden's shoulder. He seemed to be resisting her, pulling against the arm pressure, like maybe he didn't want to be hugged as much as she wanted to hug him.

''She'd been Terry's roommate, and she knew about the gun. She was also your girl friend and it had to be she who told you about it. So it was done and you were clean and all was well and then I showed up. And I talked to you about it, and you panicked. You must have called Broz the minute I left your office that day because he sent his people out to talk to me right after that. And the manuscript was returned the next day. But I kept it up and you panicked worse. Cathy Connelly could tie you to the murder. What if you broke up? What if your wife heard about her and blew the whistle on your girl friend and your girl friend talked for spite? She was the only one who knew about you and Broz. Other people maybe could tie you to SCACE, but the worst that would mean is a ''no'' decision at tenure time. The university wasn't pressing charges on the Godwulf Manuscript. If you could get rid of Cathy Connelly, you and Broz could recruit a new pusher to replace Dennis Powell and things would be going just as swell and nice as they had before. So you went and killed her. That was maybe the dumbest thing of all, because it's not your line of work and you did a terrible job. If Broz hadn't put a lot of pressure on someone you'd be sitting around in a small room at Walpole right now. And when I kept after you and you called Broz about it again, Broz must have had enough. So you thought he'd kill me, but he thought he'd kill you. And he will. You got one chance and that is to take away his reason. Tell me, tell the cops, maybe we can get Broz, but whether or not we do we can keep him from getting you . . . I think.''

''She helped me,'' he said.

Judy Hayden said, ''Lowell . . .'' in a choked voice.

''It was her idea to kill Cathy. She went with me; she held Cathy when I hit her on the head. She said to make it look as if Cathy drowned in the tub.''

Her arm dropped away from his shoulder and hung straight down by her side. She didn't look at him, or me.

Hayden went on with no animation, like a recording. ''I

don't use drugs, but many people need them to liberate their consciousnesses, to elevate their perceptions and free them from the bondage of American hypocrisy. A drug culture is the first step to an open society. I was the man who got them from Joseph Broz. Dennis supplied them to the community. He didn't know where I got them, and I didn't know where he sold them. It was just right.'' He had a dreamy little half smile on his face now as he talked, and his eyes were concentrating on a point somewhere left of my shoulder.

''Then he spoiled it. He complained about the quality. Said the heroin was cut too much. I said I'd speak to my supplier. Joseph Broz said that the quality was fine and was going to remain the way it was. Dennis threatened to tell the police on me. He threatened to bring down everything we'd worked for, everything that SCACE stood for. Simply because he wanted the heroin stronger. He sacrificed his every ideal. He betrayed the movement. He had to be executed. Miss Connelly and I discussed it and she suggested the gun. I discussed it with a representative of Joseph Broz and he said if we would give him the gun, he would manage the rest. Miss Connelly went there to visit and took the gun. It is too bad Miss Orchard has to suffer; she is a member of the movement and we bear her no ill will.''

He paused. Still looking past my shoulder. The smile was a full smile now and his eyes were shiny. In a minute he'd start addressing me as ''my fellow Americans.''

The smile faded. ''So now you know,'' he said.

''Will you tell it all to the police?'' I said.

He shook his head. ''I'll die without speaking,'' he said. Ronald Colman, Major André, Nathan Hale, the Christian martyrs.

''You're not going to die,'' I said. ''The death penalty is not legal at the moment. You will merely go to jail, unless you don't tell the cops. Then you will die without speaking like you almost did last night. Remember last night. You didn't seem so eager for silent martyrdom last night.''

Judy Hayden put her hand on his shoulder. ''Tell them, Lowell,'' she said.

He shrugged his shoulder away from her touch. ''I've told him, and that's all I'm telling anyone. You brought him here. I wouldn't have had to tell him anything if you'd not brought him here. I trusted you and you betrayed me too. Can I trust no one? You've never cared about the movement. Dennis never cared about the movement. Cathy never cared about the movement.''

''I care about you,'' she said. She was standing very stiff and very still. The palms of her hands appeared to press hard against her thighs.

''I am the movement,'' he said, and the dreamy smile was back and the eyes positively glistened. He was listening to the sound of a different drummer all right, and it was playing ''God Save the King.''

No one said anything. I didn't want to look at Mrs. Hayden. In the silence I heard a click like a key turning in the lock. I turned toward the door behind me, but I was wrong. It was the connecting door to the next room. It swung open suddenly and Phil stepped through it. In his hand was a gun with a silencer. He pointed it at me, and said in his rusty voice, ''Time's up.''

24

Phil closed the door.

"The couple in the elevator with us," I said. Phil nodded.

"You had Mrs. Hayden staked out," I said. Phil nodded again.

"I am a horse's ass," I said.

"We used five people," Phil said. "It's hard to spot."

The gun in his hand was an Army issue .45 automatic. It fired a slug about the size of a baseball and at close range would knock down a sex-crazed rhinoceros. Most people didn't use them because they were big and clumsy and uncomfortable to wear and they jumped in your hand a lot when you fired. In Phil's hand it looked natural and just right.

Hayden said, "Thank God you're here."

Phil made a movement with his lower jaw that might have been a smile. "Get over beside Spenser," he said. Hayden stared at him.

Phil's voice grated without inflection. "Move."

Hayden moved. Mrs. Hayden moved with him. Fred Astaire and Ginger Rogers. What the hell made me think of that?

"Take your gun out with two fingers of your left hand, Spenser, and drop it on the floor."

I did as he said. Since the gun was on my right hip I had to twist my body some and that made my side hurt more. In a little while it wouldn't matter.

I felt shaky, like I'd had too much coffee, and apprehension tingled along my arms. I fumbled the gun out and dropped it on the floor.

"Kick it under the bed," Phil said. Every time he talked you wanted to clear your throat. I kicked the gun.

"You can't harm me," Hayden said. "If you do and Joseph Broz hears of it you will be in very serious trouble."

Jesus, Alice in Wonderland. I was studying Phil. He was a puzzle, and that opaque white walleye didn't help any. It was hard to tell what he was looking at. He was dressed as he had been before—the coat buttoned up to the neck, the pink-tinted glasses. I watched his hand on the gun; maybe at the instant I saw the finger tighten on the trigger, I could jump him. The hammer wasn't back. Phil probably always carried a round in the chamber. That would give me an extra hundredth of a second. I wished my side weren't sore and bandaged. I felt weak, and diving across the bed and taking the gun away from Phil was not the kind of work that the weak do well. It wasn't a very big chance, but standing still while he shot me in the face was an even smaller chance. He'd shoot me first, figuring I'd be the one to give him trouble.

Hayden kept talking in a singsong voice that rose in pitch as he spoke. "Do you have any idea whom you're dealing with? Do you know how many people are in the movement? If anything happens to me they'll never rest till I'm avenged. They'll track you down and harry you out, however well hidden you may think you are. And Joseph Broz will be very angry with you."

Phil seemed interested. He'd probably never seen anything like Hayden before.

"And you know how angry Joseph Broz can be. I'm on your side. I want to change all of this. I want a world where you won't have to work outside the law. I'm not your enemy. Shoot them. He's your enemy and she is too, she betrayed me. She led him here. She led you here. Kill

178

her. Don't kill me. Please don't. Please don't.''

His legs went out from beneath him and he dropped to his knees and back onto his heels. ''Please don't. Please don't. Please don't.''

Phil liked it. He cackled to himself.

''What are you going to do to my husband?'' Mrs. Hayden asked.

Phil cackled again. ''I'm going to shoot him.''

Mrs. Hayden jumped at him. The gun made a muffled thud as Phil fired. It must have hit her, but it didn't stop her. She got hold of his gun arm with both hands and bit into his wrist. She was making a sound that was somewhere between a moan and a growl. The gun thudded again. I went over the bed at Phil. With his left forearm he cuffed me across the face. It was like running into a tree branch. I sprawled on the bed, rolled onto the floor, and came up for him again. Mrs. Hayden had her teeth sunk in his arm. He was pounding the side of her head with his left hand, and trying to get his right loose to use the gun. I got on his back this time and got my right arm around his neck. He moved away from the bed and I rode his back like a kid, wrapping my legs around his middle. I was trying to get my left hand against the back of his head and lock my right hand against my left forearm. If I could do that I could strangle him.

It was not easy to do. Phil kept his chin tucked down and I couldn't get my forearm against his windpipe. He reached backward with his left hand and got hold of my hair. He bowed his back and tried to flip me over forward. He couldn't, because I had my legs scissored around his middle. But the effort tumbled him forward and all three of us went down in a pile. Mrs. Hayden was beneath us, her teeth still sunk into Phil's forearm, her hands still clutching the gun. Phil let go of my hair with his left hand and his thumb felt for my eye. I pressed my face against his back to protect it. He had a sweaty rancid smell. I got

179

the fingers of my left hand hooked under his nostrils and pulled. He grunted and his chin came up an inch. It was enough. My right forearm slipped in against his Adam's apple. I put the right hand on the left forearm and made a pivot of it, bringing my left hand up behind his head. Then I squeezed.

I could feel the muscles in his neck bulge. It was like trying to strangle a hydrant. He gurgled and I squeezed harder. He was incredibly strong. He heaved himself up, carrying me on his back and dragging Mrs. Hayden up too. The gun thudded three more times. He tried to break the hold by lunging back against the wall and knocking me loose, but he couldn't. He clawed left-handed at my forearm, then with his fingernails. The gun thudded again and again until all eight rounds were gone. I had no idea what they were hitting. I was concentrating everything I had on strangling Phil. My whole life was invested in the pressure of my forearm on his throat.

He gurgled again and I could feel his chest heaving in the struggle to breathe. He was scratching at my forearm like he was digging for the bone. I squeezed. The blood pounded in my ears from the effort and I couldn't see anything but a dance of dust motes where my face stayed pressed against his shoulder. Phil made a noise like a crow cawing, turned very slowly in a complete turn, and fell over backward on top of me. He stopped clawing at my arm. He made no noise. He was inert. Mrs. Hayden was inert on top of both of us, her teeth still in his arm. I kept squeezing, unable to see with his back pressed against my face, unable to hear anything but the pounding in my own head, unable to feel anything but the strain of my arm against his neck. I squeezed. I don't know how long I squeezed, but it was surely for a long time after it made any difference.

When I let go I could barely open my hand. I was slippery with sweat and too tired to move right away. I lay there panting with the weight of Phil and Judy Hayden on me. When the dancing motes began to dissipate I dragged myself out from under the body.

Phil was dead. I realized that Phil and the floor and my leg were sticky with blood—Mrs. Hayden's blood. I touched her and she didn't move. I felt for her pulse. She had none. She'd bled to death hanging on to Phil's arm. Her teeth were still bitten into it. Phil had emptied his gun in desperation. There was no way to tell how many had hit her. I didn't want to know. I stood up. The room was a shambles. Blood was smeared everywhere. The night stand was tipped over. So was the television set. The bed was broken. I was aware that my side hurt. There was some blood staining my shirt. The wound had opened again.

I remembered Hayden. I looked around. I didn't see him. He was going to get few merit badges for *semper fidelis*. I started for the door. The chain lock was still on it. The door that Phil had come through locked from the other side. I went over the the bathroom. It was locked.

I said, "Hayden."

No answer. I banged on the door. Nothing. I felt crazy and hot. I backed up three steps and ran right through the door. It was thin and tore from its hinges. No Hayden. I pulled the shower curtain aside and there he was. In the tub, sitting down with his knees drawn up to his chest.

He looked at me and said, "Please don't."

I reached down, took the front of his shirt in both hands, and yanked him up out of the tub. There was a peculiar smell about him and I realized he'd wet himself. I was revolted. I swung him around, the way a trackman throws the hammer, and slung him into the bedroom. He stumbled, almost fell, and stopped, looking down at his wife. I came beside him. I took his chin in my hand and raised his head. I put my face up against his, so that our noses touched. I could barely speak and my body was shivering. I said, "I have killed three people to save your miserable goddamn ass. Your wife took about six slugs in the stomach and bled to death in great agony to save your miserable goddamn ass. I will call up Martin Quirk in a minute and he will come here to arrest you. You will tell him everything that you know and everything that I want you to tell him and everything that he asks you. If you do not I will get Quirk to put us alone together in a cell in the cellar and I will beat you to death. I promise you that I will."

He said, "Yes, sir." When I let him go he didn't move—just stood there looking down at his wife with his hands clasped behind his back. I went to the phone and dialed a number I knew too well.

• 25 •

The room was busy. The people from the coroner's office had come and taken Phil away, and Mrs. Hayden. The hotel doctor had come and rebandaged my side and told me to go in to outpatient this afternoon and have some new stitches in the wound. Beside the broken TV set Frank Belson stood in front of Lowell Hayden, who sat in the only chair in the room. Hayden was talking and Belson was writing things down as he talked. Quirk was there and three uniformed cops and a couple of plainclothes types were standing around looking shrewd and keeping an eye out for clues. The occupant of the next room had been whacked on the head and locked in a closet and was now planning to sue the hotel. The house man was trying to persuade him not to.

Quirk was as immaculate and dapper as ever. He had on a belted tweed topcoat, pale pigskin gloves.

"Not bad," he said. "He had a gun and you didn't and you took him? Not bad at all. Sometimes you amaze me, Spenser."

"We took him," I said. "Me and Mrs. Hayden."

"Either way," Quirk said.

"How about the kid?" I said.

"Orchard? I already called. They're processing her out now. She'll be on the street by the time we get through here."

"Yates?"

Quirk smiled with his mouth shut. "Captain Yates is at this moment telling the people in the pressroom about

183

another triumph for truth, justice, and the American way.''

"He's got all the moves, hasn't he?" I said.

One of the plainclothes dicks snickered and Quirk looked at him hard enough to hurt.

"How about Joe Broz?"

Quirk shrugged. "We got a pickup order out on him. How long we can keep him when we get him, you can guess as well as I can. In the last fifteen years we've arrested him eight times and made one charge stick—loitering. It will help if Hayden sticks to his story.''

I looked at Hayden, sitting in the chair. He was talking now in his deep phony voice. Lecturing Belson. Explaining in detail every aspect of the case and explaining its connection with the movement, drawing inference and elaborating implications, demonstrating significance, and suggesting symbolic meaning. Belson looked as if he had a headache. Hayden was enjoying himself very much.

"He'll stick," I said. "Imagine him lecturing a jury. Your only problem will be getting him to stop.''

The phone rang. One of the plainclothes cops answered and held it out to Quirk.

"For you, Lieutenant.''

Quirk answered, listened, said, "Okay," and hung up.

"Orchard's parents can't be located, Spenser. She says she wants you to come down and pick her up. How's your side?''

"It only hurts when I laugh.''

"Okay, beat it. We'll be in touch about the coroner's inquest.''

I looked at Hayden again. He was still talking to Belson, his rich voice rolling out and filling the room. For him, a big, homely, masculine woman had taken six .45 slugs in the stomach. The press arrived and a photographer in what looked like a leather trench coat was snapping

Hayden's picture. Hayden looked positively triumphant. *Le mouvement, c'est moi.* Jesus!

Outside the room the corridor was crowded with people. Two uniformed cops kept them at bay. As I shoved through, someone asked what had happened in there.

"It was a lover's quarrel," I said, "with the world."

I wondered what I meant. I didn't even remember where I got the phrase. Downstairs the lobby was as refined and ornate as ever. I went through it into the midafternoon sunshine. The hotel was dwarfed by the enormous insurance building that rose behind it. The sides of the skyscraper were reflecting glass and the sun off the glass was dazzling. Tallest building in Boston. Excelsior, I thought. Tower of Babel, I thought. My car was parked in front of the library. I got in and drove the short block to police headquarters. I parked out front by the yellow curb on Berkeley Street. It's the only place in the area where there are always parking spaces.

I got out of the car arthritically. When I straightened up she was outside the building, on the top step. Squinting against the light, she was wearing a dapple gray suede coat with white fur trim at collar, cuffs, hem, and down the front where it buttoned. Her hands were thrust deep in her pockets and a shoulder purse hung against her left side. She was wearing black boots with three-inch heels and looking up at her from street level she looked a lot taller than I knew she was. Her hair was loose and dark against the high white fur collar.

Neither of us moved for a minute. We stood in silence in the bright afternoon and looked at each other. Then she came down the steps.

I said, "Hi."

She said, "Hi."

I went around and opened the door to my car on her side. She got in, tucking the skirt of her long coat modestly under as she slid in. I went around and got in my side.

She said, "Do you have a cigarette?"

I said, "No. But I can stop and pick some up. There's a Liggett's on the corner."

She said, "If you would. I'd like to buy some make-up too."

I pulled over and parked in the alley between the parking garage and the drugstore at the corner of Berkeley and Boylston streets. As we got out she said, "I don't have any money, can you lend me some?"

I nodded. We went into the drugstore. It was a big one—a soda fountain down one side, bottles of almost everything on the other three walls, three wide aisles with shelves selling heating pads and baby strollers, paperback books and candy and Christmas lights. Terry bought a package of Eve cigarettes, opened it, took one out, lit it, and inhaled half of it. She let the smoke out slowly through her nose. I paid. Then we went to the make-up counter. She bought eye liner, eye shadow, make-up base, rouge, lipstick, and face powder. I paid.

I said, "Would you like an ice cream cone?"

She nodded and I bought us two ice cream cones. Vanilla for me, butter pecan for her. Two scoops. We went back out to my car and got in.

"Could we drive around for a little while?" she asked.

"Sure."

I drove on down Berkeley Street and onto Storrow Drive. At Leverett Circle I went over the dam to the Cambridge side and drove back up along the river on Memorial Drive. When we got to Magazine Beach we parked. She used the rearview mirror to put on some of the make-up. I looked across the gray river at the railroad yards. Behind them, half-hidden by the elevated extension of the Mass Turnpike, was Boston University Field, with high-rise dorms built up around the stadium. When I was a kid it had been Braves Field until the Braves moved to

Milwaukee and B.U. bought the field. I remembered going there with my father, the excitement building as we went past the ticket taker and up from the dark under stands into the bright green presence of the diamond. The Dodgers and the Giants used to come here then. Dixie Walker, Clint Hartung, Sibbi Sisti, and Tommy Holmes. I wondered if they were still alive.

Terry Orchard finished her make-up and stowed it all away in her shoulder purse.

"Spenser?"

"Yeah?"

"What can I say? Thank you seems pretty silly."

"Don't say anything, kid. You know and I know. Let it be."

She leaned forward and held my face in her hands and kissed me hard on the mouth and held it for a long time. The fresh make-up was sweet smelling. When she finished her lipstick was badly smeared.

"Gotcha," I said. "Let's go home."

We drove on out Soldier's Field Road toward Newton. She slid over in the seat beside me and put her head against my shoulder while I drove, and smoked another cigarette. There was a maroon Lincoln Continental with a black vinyl roof parked in the driveway of her house when we got there.

"My father," she said. "The police must have reached him." As I pulled up to the curb the front door opened and Terry's mother and father appeared on the porch.

"Shit," she said.

"I'll let you out here and keep going, Love," I said. "This is family business."

"Spenser, when am I going to see you again?"

"I don't know. We don't live in the same neighborhood, Love. But I'm around. Maybe I'll come by sometime and take you to lunch."

"Or buy me an ice cream," she said.

"Yeah, that too."

She stared at me and her eyes filled up.

She said, "Thank you," and got out of the car and walked up toward her house. I drove back in town, got my side stitched at Boston City by the same doctor, and went home.

It was dark when I got there and I sat down in my living room and drank bourbon from the bottle without turning on the lights. They'd given me two pills at the hospital and combined with the bourbon they seemed to kill the pain pretty well.

I looked at the luminous dial of my wrist watch, 6:45.

I felt as if I'd wrung out, and was drip-drying. I also felt that spending the night alone would have me screaming incoherently by 3 A.M.

I looked at my watch again, 6:55.

I turned the light on and took off the watch. Inside, it still said Brenda Loring, 437-3676.

I dialed the number. She answered.

I said, "Hello, my name is Spenser, do you remember me?"

She laughed, a terrific laugh, a high-class laugh. "With the shoulders, and the nice eyes, yeah, I remember." And she laughed again. A good laugh, full of promise. A hell of a laugh when you thought about it.